BAD DAY AT SAN JUAN

Black Pete Bowen had thought he was a lucky son-of-a-gun with his own silver mine, a beautiful wife and three trusty amigos, but his peace was shattered when Rámon Corral and his federales rode into town. Now he faced disaster, for his wife had been kidnapped and he and his friend, Nathan, were beaten, roped to the front of a train and sent back to the Texan frontier. But spurred on by vengeance and grim determination, he took on the vicious Corral and his federales . . .

Books by John Dyson
in the Linford Western Library:

BLACK PETE — OUTLAW
THE LAWLESS LAND
DEATH AT SOMBRERO ROCK
THE CROOKED SHERIFF
THE BLACK MARSHAL
BLOOD BROTHERS

JOHN DYSON

BAD DAY AT SAN JUAN

Complete and Unabridged

LINFORD
Leicester

First published in Great Britain in 1997 by
Robert Hale Limited
London

First Linford Edition
published 1998
by arrangement with
Robert Hale Limited
London

British Library CIP Data

Dyson, John, *1943*–
    Bad day at San Juan.—Large print ed.—
    Linford western library
    1. Western stories
    2. Large type books
    I. Title
    823.9'14 [F]

ISBN 0–7089–5326–3

Published by
F. A. Thorpe (Publishing) Ltd.
Anstey, Leicestershire

Set by Words & Graphics Ltd.
Anstey, Leicestershire
Printed and bound in Great Britain by
T. J. International Ltd., Padstow, Cornwall

This book is printed on acid-free paper

1

The village of San Juan, in the state of San Luis Potosi, was in fiesta. Since early dawn peons had been coming in from the deep valleys of the surrounding mountains, on foot or on long-suffering burros, to mingle on the plaza before the great mission church. It was the Day of the Dead. None knew that before nightfall it would become known as the Day of Death.

★ ★ ★

A tall Texan of middle years stood at the entrance to his silver mine in the hills above San Juan and drawled, 'Don't look like we'll get any work out of anybody today.' His name was Pete Bowen. He was lean and dark-complexioned, with an amused glint in his eyes. 'Nor tomorrow, neither. They'll all be hungover.'

'These Mexicans.' His young partner, Nathan Strong, ran fingers through his close-cropped blond thatch. 'Any excuse for a fiesta.'

'Ach!' Miguel was a copper-bronzed gun-fighter who had sided them for several years. 'My people need to escape the yoke of toil,' he growled. 'They need their dancing, their firewater. Today is no ordinary fiesta. Today we pay tribute to Death who hangs always over us. Today we celebrate. Tomorrow we, too, may go that way.'

'Which is his flowery way of saying he's gonna go git stuck into the booze and *señoritas*.' Nathan, a wiry fellow-Texan, grinned and fixed his blue eyes on Pete. 'We gonna give him the day off?'

Pete smiled wryly, and jerked tight the cinch on his black stallion. 'Don't rightly see how we can stop him, him bein' one of these durn greasers hisself.

You better go ask the gals if they fancy a ride into town.'

'Yee-haaugh!' Nathan punched a gloved hand with his fist. It was the news he had been waiting for. They hadn't been to town in a month or more. They had struck a fine seam and were forever busy down the silver mine hauling out ore. He strutted away like a bandy-legged bantam cock to go give Melody and Louisa the good news and hurry them up.

The mine was ten miles away from San Juan and their equipment and supplies had to be hauled up a precarious mountain trail. They had been in the vicinity a year. It had been hard work down the damp, dark shaft, but it had paid off.

Miguel, his sombrero hanging on his back, his bald head the colour of mahogany, the rat-tail remains of his black hair hanging over his shoulders, was already singing at the top of his lung-power, and making his mustang twirl in a mockery of dance, when the two girls emerged from the cabins. 'Hai-yi-yi!' He grinned at them through his moustachios, blowing kisses with his fingers. 'Mount up, *muchachas. Andale!'*

Melody, dark, with a happy, melon-like countenance, in a ruffled skirt and off-the-shoulder blouse, gave some cheeky Spanish riposte, and was swung up to sit side-saddle behind Nathan, clutching his waist.

Louisa was in a crisp blouse, calf-length culotte riding pants over boots, and a stiff-brimmed hat shadowing her delicately-carved features. She was a Creole, of Spanish aristocratic descent and, as such, cream-skinned, a rarity among Mexican women, and much admired for her beauty. She took the reins of a grey gelding Pete had brought from the stable. He put a hand to her boot and helped her swing into the saddle.

The tall Texan climbed onto his black stallion, Jesus, and flicked a finger to his hat to the Mexican cook,

Juanita, who had come to the door of one of the cabins. 'We'll be back in the morning,' he called.

And they started off down the rocky trail towards the village, a cluster of white adobe houses, that could be glimpsed way off in the valley bottom amid its green and fertile fields.

* * *

Ramón Corral was slumped in a carved oak chair in the governor's mansion in the city of San Luis Potosi, the capital of the state. A squat, sturdy man, he was in the uniform of tight, silver-embroidered grey suede of the dreaded Guardia Rural, only his was hung with numerous flashing star-medals and decorations. His coat hung open, as did his white, ruffled shirt to reveal his bull-neck and hirsute chest from which came a coarse, guttural laugh. A serving maid approached to offer him a bowl of fruit. He grabbed at her and swung her on to his knee. 'I'd prefer your peaches.'

The girl wriggled, alarmed, but afraid to resist and gave a look of appeal to the governor, Hernan Fernandez, a man of more icy demeanour. Fernandez gave her a severe smile, as if to say, let him have his way. It did not do to upset Ramón Corral, a man widely rumoured to be in line for the vice-presidency.

'The programme is for you to inspect the troops this morning, after which there will be a reception for you to meet the leading citizens of the state.'

There was a cackle of fire-crackers in the street outside as people celebrated the Day of the Dead, and Corral laughed, 'What's that? Gunfire? You have an insurrection?'

'Ours is a peaceful state,' Fernandez said. 'We no longer have any trouble with subversives or bandits.'

'No, you're the only bandit left in the state.' Corral grinned through his heavy moustache and kneaded the startled girl's breasts. 'Don't think I haven't heard how you pledged the government to give two thousand dollars to the

American companies for every mile of railroad built.'

'Well, the railroad has been built, hasn't it, going all the way through our state and south to Mexico City? And from here all the way north to the Rio Grande and the Texan border? Isn't that what *el presidente* wanted us to do? Progress. The opening up of our country, for which he has received world acclaim.'

'Sure,' Ramón drawled. 'But how much went to the railroads? And how much went into your private coffers? No, don't protest, *señor*. You have been very lavish with your concessions of public lands to the *gringo* companies. Some might say too lavish. Some might say you have been lining your own pockets.'

Fernandez gave a prim smile and adjusted his high-collared khaki uniform. 'Your Excellency misjudges me. I work only in the president's interest.'

'Ha!' Corral threw the girl away, having lost interest for the moment, reached out for a fine peach and bit into it. 'Don't worry, *señor*. You could hardly be expected to live on a governor's salary. I am governor of Sonora and how can I live on one income? That's why I have made myself head of the *rurales*. I know what goes on. Don't try to pull the wool over my eyes, that's all.'

Fernandez narrowed his eyes and nodded. 'Our beloved leader, Porfirio Diaz, personally asked me to encourage American investment in the state. You will be meeting some of our Yankee businessmen, company managers, railroad men, mining engineers, today. Of course the wheels of diplomacy have to be oiled. It is the custom. But it has not been done to the extent you suggest.'

'Shut up, you snivelling dog.' Corral's words snapped out like a bullwhip. 'Don't soft-soap me. You may be the biggest bandit in San Luis Potosi, but there's one bigger.' He tapped his chest, significantly. 'I could have you arrested and shot tonight.'

'Your Excellency, there is no need for such language. May I remind you you are here as our guest on a state visit.'

'Yeah.' The swarthy Corral got to his feet and began to button his uniform. He reached for his great sombrero, inlaid with gold and hung with silver conchos. 'Send that girl to my room at siesta. Let's get on with it.'

★ ★ ★

The five *amigos* were singing a popular Mexican ballad, 'La Ventana', Miguel strumming his guitar and shrilling the lead, the others joining in the deep wild choruses, as they went cantering along the valley past the small farmsteads. The people of San Juan counted themselves lucky they were not peons on some vast hacienda. Their valley was too narrow and rocky to be considered of much worth, and so they tilled their patches of red earth amid the bamboos, yuccas, and greenery, took

9

their produce into market to sell or barter, as they had done since time immemorial, and lived a pleasant enough life. Only the building of the railroad out on the plain hinted of changes to come.

The town was buzzing as they rode in, the narrow streets packed with people, children wearing grotesque skull masks, pedlars selling trays of sugar-icing skeletons, or garish pastry corpses peering from miniature coffins. The mission church, elaborately carved and decorated like some chipped and decaying great white wedding cake, boomed forth its bells, and out of its portals came a stream of people, led by the priest, and boys with candles. A huge tableau of Our Lady of Guadaloupe was borne out by a team of men, visible only by their hairy calves and sandalled feet beneath the covering mantle. There were so many burros tethered in the dusty plaza, and at the hitching rails outside the surrounding shops and *cantinas*, the *gringos* had difficulty finding a spot to tie their horses.

Louisa, a devout Roman Catholic, hurried off to pray in the church to Our Lady, and to follow the throng out to the cemetery where many would spend the day picnicking and carousing over the graves of their ancestors, calling to their spirits. Pete, Nathan, Miguel and Melody were more interested in alcoholic spirits, and went clomping in to Felipe's place. It was a barn of a restaurant, wondrously cool and shady after the hot sun. The only sounds were the creaking of wonky fans on the ceiling, worked by small boys with pulley ropes, the hum of conversation, and the click of chequer boards. Most folk were out on the streets.

'Howdy,' Pete muttered, as Felipe brought them tankards of iced beer, and a saucer of peppered cucumber. '*Muchas gracias, señor*. How you doin'? Big day today?'

'Things will hot up later,' Felipe said. He pushed back a chair and joined

11

them, offering cigars and lighting them. The *gringos* were popular in San Juan. They paid their labourers above the rate, which, admittedly, wasn't much, were good customers and, unlike other *Americanos*, weren't too high and mighty to talk to Mexicans. In the year they had been there they had made many friends.

While the others gossiped, Pete picked up a newspaper, printed in San Luis Potosi two days before, and browsed through it. It was interesting, occasionally, to hear what was going on in the outside world. He thrust out his long legs in their leather shotgun chaps, rested his boots on his spurs, drew on the cigar, and sighed, contentedly. He reckoned another year of working the mine and they would have enough to buy a big spread, either back in the States, up Montana way, or down in Argentina. Somewhere nobody knew him. He had an idea there were still numerous warrants extant for his arrest. The Rangers and bounty hunters did not give up easily.

His body tensed as he saw the headline: 'Minister of the Interior, Ramón Corral, to visit San Luis'.

'That butcher,' he murmured. 'I thought we'd put space between him and us.'

A shiver went through him as he took a swig of the beer and remembered how, as governor of the north-eastern state of Sonora, Corral had carried out a genocidal war against Yaqui Indians, burning their mountain villages, hanging them, or deporting them in chains to the southern jungle mines of Yucatan. Pete and his *amigos* had ridden for him at first, as hired guns, but had been so disgusted by the bloodshed they had joined the Yaqui leader, Cajeme, in the hills[1]. In the end they had escaped by crossing the jagged peaks of the central divide and

---

[1] See *Bullwhip*.

heading hundreds of miles south. Most mountain villages in Mexico were so remote some had not even heard that Diaz was their new leader. Pete had thought that in San Juan they would be far enough away from Corral's vengeance. But here the brute was again, not so very far away, reviewing the troops in the state capital that very day.

'What's the matter, *hombre*?' Nathan asked. 'You look worried.'

Pete pointed to the headline and passed the paper across. Felipe eyed the article, curiously. 'You know Ramón Corral, Mister Johnson?'

Pete, who went by the name of Johnson in these parts, nodded, moodily. 'We have met.'

Nathan gave a low whistle. 'That bastard again. He's only visiting the capital. He ain't likely to be coming up this way. Minister of the Interior now, is he? How did that ignorant pig manage that?'

'He ain't so stupid as he pretends

to be,' Pete said. 'Him and Diaz are buddies. The wolves dividing the spoils.' He gave a scoffing grin at the picture of the benevolent 'father of the country' upon the wall. 'Diaz certainly knows how to clamp down the iron fist on this country. He uses men like Ramón Corral who are as ruthless as he.'

Felipe looked around over his shoulders, worried, beckoning to them with outstretched fingers, like a piano player, to lower their voices. 'It is not wise to say these things,' he hissed.

Even Miguel's eyes flickered with concern. 'Something tell me maybe it time to move on. I got a bad feeling.'

'Relax, you guys,' Melody put in. 'It says Corral is busy inspecting the troops at San Luis today. and, if I know him, he will be even busier getting drunk and chasing the girls. He's like Miguel.'

'This ain't no joking matter, hon,' Nathan chided her. 'Personally, I won't feel safe 'til I'm back in Texas, an' even there's hot enough. Maybe Miguel's right, maybe it's time to mosey back. Ain't we got enough stashed away yet, Pete?'

'We got a good wad in the bank. But it seems a shame to leave the rest of that seam. Man don't strike pure silver like that often in his lifetime.'

'Aw, we weren't cut out to spend our lives scrabbling around in dark holes. We're cowboys. I say it's time to go.'

'Hang on! Pete's got a point,' Melody said. 'You've got legal title to this mine. Even if it is under assumed names. Nobody hurts Americans in Mexico. They are our great leader's honoured guests, encouraged to bring their trade to our country. Why, you're treated better than bullfighters.'

Pete grinned and eased the twin, pearl-handled Smith and Wessons in his gunbelt. 'If we go back up to the mine and keep out of the limelight I don't see as how anyone's going to wise up to us. Six months more and we can double our money. It'll make all the difference.'

'This Corral,' Nathan asked, 'is he still governor of Sonora?'

'*Si*,' Felipe nodded. 'That is too good an income to give up. But he is also in charge of security for the whole country. The man at the head of the *federales* and *rurales*, and a network of spies, the man at the top of the pyramid.'

'The pyramid that grinds you all down.' Nathan pointed to the picture on the wall. 'Yeah, I know, *don't* say it, not with him listening.'

'Let's change the subject,' Pete said, tucking the newspaper under a pile as he saw Louisa enter the restaurant. 'This is s'posed to be a fiesta, for Christ's sake! Felipe, what's on the menu? Something special?' He added, in a low voice, 'Don't say anything about this to my wife.'

★ ★ ★

'If that greasy swine had any more medals he'd have to pin 'em on his arse,' one of the Americans chuckled, as they watched Ramón Corral swagger about the reception at San Luis Potosi. 'He sure ain't got no more room on his chest.'

Corral spun round on his spurred high boots, his puffy eyes blazing like an angry boar about to charge. 'You say something, *señor*?' The room fell so quiet they could hear the chandeliers tinkling in the breeze. Corral strode forward and planted himself, hands on hips, before the man who had made the remark. 'What do you do, *meester*?' He slurred the last word like an insult.

'I'm an engineer . . . a mining engineer,' the man replied. He was rattled by Corral's defiant gaze, but pulled himself together. 'Union Copper and Silver Company. You must have heard of us.'

'Yeah. That reeng a bell, like you say.' Corral put out his thick paw and squeezed the hesitantly offered hand. Or crunched would be a better word. The American, no small man, gritted his teeth as the bear grip closed harder and harder, Corral's muddy eyes glimmering into his own. He almost gasped as Corral released him. 'An' how you doin'? You found much silver?'

'So, so.' The American shrugged, easing his fingers. 'We ain't done too bad. Not as well as that feller up country.'

'Up country?'

'Yep. Up in the mountains behind San Juan. Rumour is he's struck big. High quality ore. Some guy called Johnson. And his partner, Nathan Williams. We're thinking of making them an offer.'

'An offer? Why so?'

'Why? Because my firm's got the capital, the means to bring in heavy equipment. Them two Texans only a coupla amateur prospectors. It's always the way. They strike lucky. We buy 'em out.'

'Texans?' Corral's dark eyes flickered like a fire's embers breaking into life. 'What they like? These two?'

'Aw, like Texans. Cowboys. They only got a basic experience of mining. Pete Johnson picked his up when he was down the Comstock shaft for a few weeks in Virginia City.'

'Pete?'

'Yeah. That's his name.' The American wished he hadn't said anything. Maybe this minister of the interior was interested in making a bid for the mine, himself. 'He's a nice enough fella, but it's time a big professional company like our'n moved in. Small-time operation's a waste of time.'

'You don' say, *señor*?' Corral stroked his chin with gold-beringed fingers, the light flashing on his decorated chest. 'What he look like, this Pete?'

'Aw, I dunno.' The American shifted awkwardly, glancing at his compatriots. 'Like a Texan. Tall, thick black hair, lazy drawl. Carries two S and W's cross-hung. He's got a peach of a wife, aristocratic Spanish girl.'

'Aristocratic?' Corral licked his lips, hungrily, at the memory of Louisa strapped naked across her horse. 'Light-skinned Creole girl?'

'Yeah, very nice.'

'And his partner? Thees Meester Williams? He short, wiry, blond hair?'

'That's right. You know them?'

'Sure as hell I know them. Who else they got there?'

'Why? What's all this about? Who the hell you think you're interrogating?'

The swarthy Corral grinned, whipped a revolver from inside his double-breasted uniform, spun it on one finger, and up-ended the barrel beneath the American's nose. 'How you like I geev you a reward? Ordered from Samuel Colt's firm. Pure inlaid gold. Two thousand dollar it cost me. You want?'

'Nope.' The American swallowed a lump in his throat. He gently pressed the barrel aside with his forefinger. 'I ain't interested in guns.'

21

'Who else?'

'Hell knows. I only met them once. Johnson, his wife, and Williams, and some greaser, I mean Mexican, hard-looking, bald head, poncho, bristling with guns. I figured him for the protection. And some gal, Mex, too. Pretty. Melody I think they called her. That's all I know.'

'*Señor!*' Corral burst into guttural laughter and slapped the engineer so hard on his shoulder his drink spilled. 'They are my friends. Good friends. Melody and Louisa. Yeah, thass right. *Muchas gracias, señor.* Enjoy your stay in *Meh-i-co.*'

Corral jerked his head at the governor and led the way to his office. He slumped in Fernandez's chair, put his spurred boots up, bit off the point of a cigar, spat it out, and said, 'I got to go.'

'Why?' Fernandez protested. 'You have a full programme. Luncheon. Your speech to make. The bullfight. The ball.'

'I want a train made ready to transport me and one hundred of my *rurales* and their horses, to the nearest halt to San Juan. And I want it quick.'

'But, why, Señor Corral?' A bead of sweat was trickling from Fernandez's close-cropped head. 'As governor I have a right to know.'

'Right? Pah! You dolt. Just do as I say. OK, I tell you. You, my friend, have been harbouring four criminals in your state. Criminals with the death penalty on their heads. This *gringo*, this Texan, he, I am sure, is Pete Bowen, convicted *in absentia* of the murder of the *jefe politico* of Sonora, Colonel Ferdinand Veraco. Not only did he shoot him, he bull-whipped him mercilessly beforehand. His two side-kicks, this Miguel and this, this Nathan so-called Williams, are fast guns responsible for the deaths of several of my soldiers. And the girl, Melody, without doubt drowned to death in his own swimming bath one of Sonora's richest landowners, General Don Ignacio Lazar. All fought as hired guerillas for the rebel Yaqui Indians against our Mexican Government.'

'My God!' Hernan Fernandez's monocle fell from his eye. 'That is quite an indictment.'

'So? The train.' Corral snapped his fingers. 'We go. We kill them.'

'Yes.' Fernandez mopped his brow. 'First, sir, I must beg caution. Let us look at the documents on this man I know as Johnson. I have them at hand somewhere. Their application to open the mine. As far as I remember he seemed a respectable married man. A former rancher and lawman. Marshal of Abilene, Dodge City and Virginia City at various times. His partner, Williams, was a US federal agent responsible for breaking a big forgery ring. I mean, they have very impressive records. You say his real name is Stone?'

'Yeah,' Coral snarled. 'And they're both outlaws, too. They ride both sides. Respectably married? Huh! Louisa

Varga. Long have I wanted to get my hands on her. She will not die, I assure you. She, I promise you, will be mine.'

'*Si, Si,* Your Excellency. The Mexicans are nothing. You can do with them as you want. But do you not think you should consult *el presidente*? Hasn't he constantly stressed that Americans are our friends and allies, that no harm must befall any one of them while they are in our country?'

'Maybe so,' Corral grunted. 'But mistakes can be made. And, then, pah, it is too late.'

'Nonetheless, I think we should telegraph Mexico City. As governor of the state I need clearance.'

Corral jumped to his feet and backhanded Fernandez across his nose, knocking him down. 'You miserable whelp. Who you think you are? You won't be governor much longer if you go against me. Have you no pride, no sense of honour? These *gringo* bandits committed horrendous crimes against most important people. They must be put down.'

Fernandez got to his feet, blood trickling from one nostril. 'I'll see about the train. It should be ready in one hour.'

'Good. That gives me time for that little *poblana*. Where is she? In the kitchens? Send her to me. A soldier should never go into battle without a good — ' The last word was lost as he slammed out of the door.

'*Merde!*' the governor said, French being the language of diplomacy. 'That man will be the death of me.'

2

The festival of San Juan was in full swing. In the late afternoon many of the peons left the cemetery and the flower-bedecked graves and returned to the town plaza where there were stalls selling all manner of sickly sweets and sherbets, a wheel of fortune to bet on, and a crude funfair, swingboats, and a gaudy, creaking carousel propelled by steam. In short, a good time was being had by all.

The *cantinas* were packed with drunken men, and women, too, high on corn beer, mescal and cheap, virulent *aguardiente*. Felipe's bar was no exception. He had pushed back the chairs and tables to make room for dancing as a five-piece combo, aptly named The Enemies of Silence, started up. Guitar, mandolin, bow fiddle, drum, and pan pipes were played expertly and with vigour by the long-haired musicians in their striped serapes and straw sombreros. The rhythms, pounded out to their shrill singing, reminded Pete of invading horsemen, or yipping Indians. And the peons swayed back and forth to them as if in a trance.

Louisa clung to him, warm and sticky with perspiration, as he swung her around in a slow sort of waltz, his hands fondling her ample buttocks, her belly and breasts pressed close. 'Oh, Pete,' she murmured. 'I love you so. Can't we go have siesta someplace?'

'Sure,' he said, and grinned as he saw Nathan and Melody doing a buckaroo's hop about the floor. 'It's sure some party.'

Not to be outdone Miguel came crashing into the bar on his mustang, pulling his heavy Dragoon revolver from his belt and firing into the ceiling, helping himself to a bottle from the counter, and tipping it back. He shook his bald head as it hit him, and gulped more down

'He's sure putting one on.' They struggled out of the throng of entranced, dark-hewn faces, and slumped down on to an old horsehair sofa in the corner. 'And I ain't doin' so bad.' He raised his bottle of mescal to her.

'Take it easy, Pete.' Louisa snuggled into him and kissed him. 'Don't want you passing out on me.'

'Aw, a man's gotta have a little drink now and again.'

She smiled as she watched the dancing, listened to the cacophony. Miguel was showing off on his horse, making it dance, raise its forehoofs, spiritedly. 'Look at him. You got good friends, Pete. We make a good team. I'm so glad we came to this place. The people are so friendly. I have never been so happy.'

'Yeah, an' we're gittin' rich, too.'

'Darling, come on, we go upstairs.'

'You sound like one of them goodtime gals, not a church-going married lady.'

'It's been so good since you . . . since you rescued me. I can't help loving you. I can't get enough of you.'

'Yeah.' He put his hand behind her slim neck and kissed her lips. 'Same goes for me. We sure have had a wonderful time this past year.' But his jaw hardened with a haunted look as he studied her. 'Come on. We paid for that bed. It's siesta time.'

For moments he thought of his first wife, and the other Spanish girl in Arizona, both of whom he had loved, both of whom had been taken from him by death.

★ ★ ★

Ramón Corral sat in the monotonously clattering train as it went across the plain. Clouds of steam floated by the window. It was a pity about the *pablona*. Why did she have to scream and beg for mercy? Just because she was a virgin and had a fiancé. What was the big deal? He had had to hit her to shut her up. He just didn't know his own strength. He had made a bit of a mess of her face. He was a Mexican and prided himself on his gallantry. He didn't want to hit a woman. Sometimes it was necessary, that was all. But he was not like that *jefe politico*, Veraco, the *gringo* had killed. That man really enjoyed torturing women, watching an old man being flayed to the point of death. Sometimes it had to be done, but, 'Ach!' he slapped at a fly on his forehead.

Revenge, however, would be sweet. It would be good to watch the Texans die, the slower the better. They were as crafty as wolves, and as fast as lightning with their guns. But what could they do against one hundred rifles?

Melody? Well, she was a pretty little *chiclera*. Maybe he would let her live, toss her into one of his Sonoran brothels.

Louisa? It was as if an icicle pierced his heart as he thought of her. What couldn't a man do with a woman like that? What a prize to have a beautiful light-skinned Creole as his wife! And it was rumoured she had aristocratic blood. If he were to be vice-president, if he were to mingle in international society, he would need a woman like that by his side. He would be good to her, woo her, offer her his fortune. And if she refused? A few cracks of the bullwhip would make her see sense. It usually did.

The big locomotive pulled up on the plain by a water tower near a ticket and telegraph office. The horses were unloaded from the goods vans, milling about in the dust. The village of San Juan was fifteen miles away up in the hills. Ramón Corral gave his orders and on his white thoroughbred, part Arab, part Spanish, went charging proudly away at the head of his platoon of one hundred *rurales* in their grey uniforms and tall sombreros, their blood-red capes draped across their blanket rolls. Corral had swapped his medallioned uniform for a more practical leather jacket, a short-barrelled carbine strapped across his back, and several bands of bullets wrapped around his sturdy frame. At heart he was a bandit, and so were most of his men, the scum of the prisons, personally recruited by him. By serving him they were rewarded with the best of food and drink, fast horses and the licence to kill. Spurs and harness jingling, eager as their wild-eyed mustangs for some action, they raised a plume of dust as they followed the telegraph wire towards the blue, mist-enfolded hills.

* * *

Black Pete, as some folk called him, pulled on his jeans, boots, and chaps in the spacious bedroom above the restaurant, and stood, bare-chested, watching his wife sleep. The calmness of her countenance was suddenly broken as she began to whimper and cry out, her body writhing, her fingers clutching the sheet. As he went to her she surfaced awake with a small scream. 'You're all right,' he said, holding her. Her brown eyes stared like a frightened antelope.

'I was back there,' she breathed. 'It was horrible.'

He knew what she meant. The recurring nightmare of the cellar in which she had been locked by the *jefe politico*, fighting off the rats that scrabbled about her in the darkness. She still bore the scars of their bites on her body. She had not had the nightmare for a long while. He had thought she was over it.

'I am frightened,' she said, hanging on to him. Her black hair rilled down like a smooth, shining waterfall to the uptilted nipples of her bare breasts. 'I have a terrible feeling we are going to be torn apart. Oh, Pete, I could not live without you.'

'Don't worry,' he said, soothing her, but a frown creased his brow. 'Maybe Miguel is right. We should head back to the States. We've got enough to start a small spread up Montana way.'

People were still partying noisily down below and out in the square, but he became alert as he heard another noise. It sounded like the drumming of horses' hooves, and sharp yipping cries. He stepped over to the window and saw them come swirling in, leaping over market stalls, knocking produce flying, the *rurales* on their wild-eyed, sweated-up mustangs, rifles in their hands. And among them the unmistakable figure of Ramón Corral.

'Jeez,' he whispered. 'He didn't waste much time.' He pulled on his cotton shirt and reached for his gunbelt. 'Get dressed.'

'Why? What's wrong?' Her face paled as she saw him standing by the window, raising the Smith and Wesson in his hand. She began to tremble with fear as she stood, naked, trying to do as he said, pull on her cotton pantalets and bodice. 'Who is it?'

'It's him. Corral.'

'Oh, my God!' she cried.

Pete had not brought his rifle, not expecting trouble, but with his revolver he could have had an easy shot out of the open window at Corral. He was sitting on his horse directly below him. Pete was very tempted to kill him, taking a bead on him double-handed with the revolver. Maybe he should have, maybe he *would* have, if it had only been him there alone. But he did not want to give their position away. 'I gotta get you outa here,' he said.

But how?

An old woman pointed towards Felipe's bar as Corral questioned her. The *rurale* chief jumped from his white horse and, with a band of his men, disappeared beneath the colonnade below the window. Others prowled on horseback about the plaza, some climbing to rooftops to cover the village. There was little chance of getting out.

'Hurry,' he hissed.

36

Louisa bundled up the rest of her clothes and they stepped out cautiously onto the tiled roofwork of the colonnade that ran along the side of the row of two-storey adobe houses.

'Come on,' he said and, at a crouch, made his way along the roof towards adjoining apartments. 'Our horses are that way. It's a hell of a drop. I don't see how we're gonna git down.'

Suddenly there was a shout. One of the *rurales* had spotted them. Bullets began to chisel into the adobe walls about them. Pete knelt and returned fire. There were not many men could shoot double-handed with accuracy, apart from Bill Hickok, but he was one of them, and three of the *rurales* were tumbled from their horses. 'Damn!' Pete gritted out. He might as well have shot Ramón Corral.

Corral, himself, had burst into the restaurant below. The first man he saw was Miguel, his bald head blackened by sun, swirling his prancing horse around.

37

'Hold it right there,' he shouted in Spanish.

Drunk as a skunk he might be, a bottle of mescal in his hand, but Miguel instantly dropped it, went for the converted Dragoon in his belt, brought it out and fired wildly. Corral's carbine blasted him out of the saddle.

Nathan, almost equally intoxicated, was slow-dancing with Melody at the back of the crowd. 'Let's get outa here,' he shouted and, hanging on to her, went charging towards the restaurant window, leaping and crashing through it. They landed on a table in the colonnade, smashing bottles and glasses, and went rolling away together.

Nathan was back on his feet, running towards his horse, Melody scampering after him. In her flounced skirt and blouse she had no gun with her. Suddenly they were confronted by a line of five *rurales* silhouetted against the harsh sunlight at the end of the colonnade. Nathan crouched ready to fan his Lightning's hammer, but they were holding their fire.

He spun around, protecting Melody with his body, and saw another five *rurales* at the other end, rifles pointed unerringly at them. And more were moving in towards them from across the plaza. They hadn't got a hope in hell. Maybe, if he had been alone, he would have gone down in a blaze of gunfire, and taken a few with him. But, maybe they would let his girl live. He tossed the Lightning away and slowly raised his hands.

'What are you doing?' Melody screamed, as she saw the gold-glinting grins of the *rurales*. 'I would rather die.' She knew they would give her little mercy.

One of the *rurales* stepped forward, jabbed his rifle into Nathan's guts, and cracked the butt up against his jaw. Nathan groaned as he sank to the ground, gasping as their boots thudded into him, into his face, into his body, boot-heels trampling him. He put out a hand, trying to clutch at Melody as she was dragged away.

Pinned down on top of the colonnade by a hail of fire from rooftops and windows, his ammunition all but gone, Pete suddenly spied below a wooden-wheeled, crudely-built peasant's cart filled with hay. 'Look,' he shouted. 'Jump for it.' Taking her hand he pulled her soaring through space to tumble safely into the hay and scramble down. He led her dodging through carts, tables, people, and burros. He reached Jesus, and vaulted on to the black stallion's broad back, pulling the loose-hitched reins free, dragging him around, swinging Louisa up behind him, and digging in his rowels.

The stallion leaped forward and Pete fired point blank into the face of a *rurale* who was pointing his rifle. He went galloping away down the street. Their only chance was to reach the mountains. Suddenly a crashing volley of rifle fire burst out from a gang of *rurales* guarding the street corner.

Jesus gave a screaming whinny and ploughed into the dust. Louisa was thrown rolling clear, but Pete was trapped by one leg beneath his horse, whose life was ebbing away in an ever-increasing pool of blood.

3

Ramón Corral sat in Felipe's restaurant, beaming at his men, biting into a slice of juicy water melon, spitting out the pips contemptuously, as he surveyed the two Texans before him, and their women, restrained to one side by his men.

Pete could hardly stand on his injured ankle and supported himself on the bar. His dark eyes, like thorns, cut into Corral. 'Waal, you got us. What you gonna do with us now?'

'What you theenk? You feelthy Yankee murderers. Tomorrow we gonna streeng you both up in public, let the people see justice be done. To do that straight away would be too kind to you. And today is fiesta. We got to play with you a leetle first.'

Nathan was half-kneeling, unable to see out of one eye, his face a bloody mess, gripping one hand to his cracked ribs. 'That figures,' he managed to grit out. 'We ain't half the murderers you scum are.'

Corral gave a great roar of laughter, and flicked the melon rind at him. 'You will suffer more for that remark. And you, too, Texan, for all the brave *rurales* you have killed.'

'Let them rot in hell. You, too,' Pete growled.

'First we have a little business for you to witness,' Corral said. 'We have the banker and the head man of the village here. They will witness you sign over the deeds of your mine to me.'

'No, your excellency,' Felipe interjected, going to stand humbly before Ramón Corral. 'This is not right. These *gringos* are good men, much loved and respected in San Juan. You should not do this to them without a proper trial.'

'You say so? You tell me my business?' Corral's nostrils flared as he raised his carbine and shot Felipe down as if he were a stray dog. Felipe went slithering back across the floor, blood oozing from the hole in his chest. 'He obviously has not heard who I am,' Corral smiled. 'Anyone else want to argue for these *much-loved* men?'

The peons stood staring, hangdog, some still in their skeletal fiesta costumes, their feathered hats, much sobered now. It was the Day of the Dead. And Death had struck. Their weather-worn faces registered no emotion. They accepted their lot, resignedly. Only Felipe's wife sobbed over him.

'Get that corpse and his whore out of here before he stinks up the place,' Corral said. He glanced at Miguel's prone figure. 'And that other one.'

One of the *rurales* bent over Miguel and snarled, 'He's not dead.'

'Well, throw him out on to the sidewalk. If he lives he lives. If he dies he dies. He is a good fighter. If he comes round maybe I will give him a job with us. We will need some new recruits thanks to the Yankees here. He will have two choices, like you all had. *Pan ó palo.*'

'I ain't a Yankee,' Pete growled. It was a sore point with him. He had fought for the Southern cause. 'What you gonna do with my wife?'

'Guess?' Corral gave an oily grin, as he bit into a carcase of cold chicken, tore it apart. 'I'm going to take her as my bride.'

'Pete is already married to me,' Louisa cried.

'Well, tomorrow you will be a widow, won't you? 'But' — he waved his hand, dismissively — 'I can assure you you are not legally married. That wily priest, Brother Francisco, was not entitled to perform the ceremony. He had been excommunicated for supporting the rebels, the Yaquis, for preaching communism. Your so-called marriage is void.'

'What happened to that priest?' Pete asked.

'He's dead. We shot him.'

Pete thought of the good Francisco and gave a grimace. What had happened, he wondered, to his little bat-eared dog? He did not know that each day he guarded the spot where his master had been martyred, that the people secretly cared for him, gave him titbits, as he whimpered beneath that wall each night waiting for his master's return. Somehow the little dog had caught the people's imagination, giving them hope and faith that one day this tyranny would pass.

'So, the head man will perform the civil ceremony.' Corral snapped his fingers, beckoning for Louisa to be dragged forward. She was still in her undergarments, her breasts partially exposed, but she shook her head, defiantly. 'No!'

'You fat bastard, you can't do this. We are important people in America. There will be an international outcry.' It was a desperate bluff. Once they had been reasonably important, but now they were just outlaws.

'You no-good saddletrash, thassall you are.' Corral rubbed it in, thumping his chest. 'You should know that *I* am the important one. *I* can do as I wish.'

He grinned as his men dragged the protesting Louisa forward, as the head man, quaking in his shoes, read out the civil marriage ceremony. Louisa's hand was gripped, and she was forced to sign the document.

'Now we all go to church,' Ramón Corral smiled. 'Bring them.'

A revolver to his head the priest chanted the marriage vows as a congregation of *rurales* and peons watched. 'Why?' Louisa screamed, staring at Pete. 'Why are they doing this to us?'

He shook his head, stunned.

'Ah, my best man, Meester Bowen. Have you got the ring? No, OK, I will use one of my own.' Corral forced his thick gold and diamond ring upon her finger, gripping her head and whispering in her ear, 'You say, *Si* I might let him live.'

'Louisa,' the priest intoned, as the cold steel pressed to his temple. 'Do you take this man, Ramón, as your husband?'

She stared, desperately, at Pete and said, coldly, '*Si*.'

'No!' Pete shouted and one of the guards' fists slammed into his temple.

'Don't knock him unconscious. I want him to sign as witness, so there will be no doubt.' And Pete was physically forced to scrawl a pen across the document.

'Caramba!' Corral mockingly cried. 'Is that not nice? Now I kees the bride.'

Louisa tried to break away as Corral pressed his stinking mouth upon hers. She wiped her lips with the back of her hand and spat.

Ramón Corral looked hurt. 'For that they will suffer more. Soon, young lady, you will learn. Come, now we watch the sport.'

The sport commenced by dragging

Melody out to the plaza where she was stood on a crate, the big Wheel of Fortune was set spinning and the *rurales* placed bets to win her. They fired their revolvers to try to make her fall off the box, and roared their laughter as bullets hammered into the backboard. One nicked her neck and blood trickled down her throat and into the cleft of her bosom.

'Ai, yi, yi!' Corral shouted. 'Who is the lucky man, who is going to lick that blood off? Hey, you! *Gringo!* Wass your name? Nathan, you wan' to bet?'

Nathan peered through his half-closed eyes, dully, as some huge brute of a *rurale* got lucky and won his girl. He watched him whoop, toss her over his shoulder and bear her off to the straw of the livery.

'After he has had his fun with her she will go to one of my brothels for my troops,' Corral genially explained. 'They are well guarded. She will never get out alive. But, first, for the rest of our sport.'

He clapped his hands, and lariats went spinning through the air over the two Americans' shoulders. Two *rurales* dug in their spurs and went charging away across the plaza on their mustangs, whipping them hard, screaming as they rode. Pete and Nathan were dragged bouncing through the dust.

'We call this the *gringo* run,' Corral grinned at Louisa. 'It ensures they don't come back to our country.' He cheered as the two riders reached the edge of the village and came galloping back across the flinty ground. 'This is better than the bullfight.'

Twice they repeated this tactic, Pete and Nathan trying to hang on to the rope to take the strain. Their leather chaparejos took much of the brunt, but the shirts of their upper bodies were ragged and blood-streaked. Their faces were hardly recognizable under the dust.

Ramón Corral strolled over, puffing on a long cigar. He put his boot into them for good measure. 'You theenk they had enough? OK. Throw them in the jail. Tomorrow they die.'

Louisa stared, horrified, as they were dragged away.

'Right,' Corral shouted to his men. 'It is fiesta. Tonight this town is yours. You dance, you get drunk. You have any girls and women you want. If anybody resists, you kill them.' He turned to the staring peasants. 'You hear that? Fiesta! You give us good time.'

The merry-go-round started up again, its oom-pah-pah music blaring out. As night fell the *rurales* staggered from *cantina* to *cantina*. The darkness was filled with screams and revolver shots. San Juan would remember this Day of the Dead.

'Why you so glum?' Corral chided Louisa. He sat stuffing himself with food and wine at a table set up in the colonnade. 'You should be happy. This is our wedding night. You can call me Ramón from now on.'

He took her up to the room above the restaurant, threw her on the bed where she had lain that afternoon with Pete. 'You be nice to me,' Corral grunted, as he undressed and fell on top of her, slobbering and groping. 'Or would you rather I throw you into a cellar filled with rats? Remember?'

He swigged at a bottle of mescal as he strove to thrust himself into her. She shuddered and lay as cold as the grave, praying to Our Lady of Guadaloupe. She closed her eyes, like some martyred saint. 'You may have my body,' she hissed out. 'But you will never have me.'

Corral was so drunk he was soon snoring in sleep. Louisa torn and sick at heart, eased herself away. She reached up to his revolver in its gunbelt hooked over the bed-head. One of these nights, she vowed, she would kill him. First she would see if he would honour his promise to let Pete live.

In their dark cell in the jailhouse

the two Americans lay stretched out on the floor.

'This is some mess we're in, eh, amigo?' Nathan whispered, trying to roll a cigarette with his raw fingers.

Pete groaned, as he listened to the noises in the night outside dying away. 'We sure ain't been in one worse.'

'What're we gonna do?'

'Beats me.'

* * *

Louisa was dressed and sitting aloof among the *rurale* lieutenants when Ramón Corral went down to the breakfast table the next morning. At first he was jovial, squeezing her hand and winking at his men. 'I know how to bring roses to your cheeks my little Louisa eh? Today we will ride out to look at my new mine. You will show me the way.'

His attention was drawn to the telegraph from the president, Porfirio Diaz, himself:

DO NOT EXECUTE THE TWO AMERICANS.
STOP.BOWEN AND STRONG MUST
BE DEPORTED TO ANSWER CHARGES
AGAINST THEM IN THE USA.STOP.REPEAT,
THEY MUST NOT BE KILLED.STOP.ANY
SUCH ACTION COULD CAUSE INTER-
NATIONAL CRISIS AT THIS TIME OF
DELICATE NEGOTIATIONS BETWEEN OUR
TWO COUNTRIES.STOP.YOU MUST DO AS
I SAY IF YOU VALUE MY FRIENDSHIP
AND YOUR JOB.STOP.

Corral kicked over the table loaded with fruits, tortillas, and coffee, startling Louisa. 'Shee-it!' he snarled. 'OK. Mark this.' He pointed a finger at her. 'I am letting them live.'

He picked up a coiled bullwhip and went stomping over to the jail. 'You will get what you gave the *jefe*,' he told them.

Pete and Nathan were hauled out and tied to a tree in the morning sunshine, as a crowd gathered. Ramón Corral sent the whip whistling and cracking across their backs, cutting through what remained of their shirts.

'Carry on,' he shouted, tossing the whip to one of his men. 'Lay on with a will. Twenty lashes each. I want to see blood. And bring out my wife to watch.'

The two Texans gritted their teeth to try not to scream out, as the rawhide cracked, flaying their backs. They gasped and shuddered when it was done. They were thrown over mules and Corral said to Louisa, 'Get on your horse. You are coming with us. We are taking them back to the railroad. You can wave goodbye to your friends.'

Amid the *rurales* they went cantering away across the plain leaving the people of San Juan to mourn their new dead and their ravished daughters.

'Tie them to the cowcatcher,' Corral ordered, and watched as the half-dead Texans were lifted on to the front of the locomotive and bound tight. 'No, don't give them any water. Nor hats. If they die from the sun that is not my business.'

He gave the engineer his orders, to steam 900 miles north to Cuidad Juárez and hand the *renegados* over to the authorities in El Paso on the other side of the frontier. 'They are welcome to them.'

He went to the front of the engine as it began shunting out jets of smoke into the sky, and the great wheels began to turn. He took off his sombrero and bowed, mockingly. '*Adios, señors*. If you ever come back to Mexico I will kill you. Pleasant journey.'

Louisa sat her horse, petrified, as she watched the two men tied to the cowcatcher, watched the train move along the track, heard its whistle, the mournful clanging of its bell. Only the whiteness of her knuckles as she gripped her reins revealed her emotion. 'Now, my dear,' Corral smiled, as he mounted up. 'Perhaps life will be more peaceful around here from now on.'

4

Yanqui Bandidos — this was scrawled in crimson paint on a board above the heads of the two Texans. And on the cowcatcher below their feet another sign read, *Murderers*. On and on the locomotive churned, smoke blasting from its tall stack, its warning bell clanging in their ears, on across plain and mountain, on through Concepción del Oro to Saltillo, branching west to Torreon across the state of Coahuila, and on north into the vastness of Chihuahua, sometimes stopping to take on water and fuel, sometimes being shunted backwards and forwards for no apparent reason, but again forever onwards following the 900 miles of single track towards the United States border. How long they were roped to the front of the engine, whether one day and night, or two, or more, Pete and Nathan were unaware for they were barely conscious.

When the train pulled into Jimenez the customary jeering crowd of children and peons gathered to peer at them. But on this occasion an old woman, her face as gnarled as a pickled walnut, in widow's eternal black, pushed through to look at them. She had a stone jar of water in her hand. She removed the corncob stopper and climbed up between the two men. She tipped the jar to Nathan's and then to Pete's lips. 'Here, my son, drink,' she said. 'I don't care what you have done. No man should be treated like this.'

'*Gracias, madre,*' Pete whispered through his cracked lips, receiving the blessing of the cool water trickling into his throat. He well knew that the old woman could be shot for doing this, as did she.

On they went, on along the eastern flank of the great mountain spine that sweeps from Alaska to the Horn, on towards El Paso. Another 150 miles and the train eased in to the city of Chihuahua. There was the customary commotion of pedlars and passengers and a detachment of soldiers, mostly solemn-faced *mestizos* or, mulattos in coarse khaki, ranging themselves with their rifles along the length of the train. Two climbed on to the cow-catcher alongside the Texans. Over the next 200 miles to the border they would be passing through bandit territory and the most feared *bandido* of all, Ignacio Parra, was believed to be in the vicinity.

They were fifty miles along the track when the soldiers' fears became reality. A horde of horsemen, white with dust, came charging as if out of nowhere, sweeping in from out of the desert to gallop alongside the rattling carriages and goods wagons, their great sombreros bent backwards by the wind. They were yelling like Apaches and firing off rifles and revolvers as they rode.

Bullets whanged and ricocheted off the boiler as they caught up with the gasping locomotive. Pete was hardly aware of what was happening, except that one of the soldiers was clawing hold of him, or trying to, gradually slipping away, mortally injured. The other guard was returning fire desperately, but, totally exposed, he, too, was pitched from his perch, not before killing two of the horsemen.

The *bandidos* could spare a few casualties. There must have been a hundred of them and most, although shooting from the saddle, were skilled marksmen. The guards, particularly those in the open wagons, were swatted like flies. On the locomotive roared at open throttle, its lever rods churning. Uncaring of their lives the bandits closed in on their prey like a huge pack of howling wolves. One galloped in alongside the tender, loosed his boots from his stirrups and leapt daringly through space to hang on and haul himself up. He covered the engineer and fireman with his revolver and soon the iron wheels had locked. The train was grinding and squealing to a halt.

The *bandidos* looked like ghosts as they rode backwards and forwards through the clouds of dust and smoke, the flash and crash of their weapons putting the passengers into a state of panic, and some of the soldiers, too, who foolishly jumped down, raised their hands ready to surrender. With wild yells of triumph the men on horseback shot them down.

Some climbed on to the roofs of the carriages and were stomping back and forth. Others fought their way inside and were taking out the last of the soldiers at close quarters. Soon khaki-clad corpses were hanging like sacks of flour from the windows, or slumped in glassy-eyed attitudes of death. Several civilians also caught stray lead. As the shooting gradually ceased there was a sudden silence punctuated by the groans of the injured and dying.

Ignacio Parra, himself, had gone strutting along the track with his lieutenants, looking for the strong room. He had expected the train to be carrying a consignment of silver from San Luis Potosi. There was a great deal of cursing when it was discovered that this was not the case. It appeared he had lost many of his men for little gain. When he saw a blood-streaked soldier struggling to raise himself from the dust he pulled his revolver and shot him dead without a second thought. Take no captives was his golden rule. Spare no man who bore arms against him for if he did one day he might live to regret it.

The peons he had no grudge against, being one himself before turning to banditry. Nonetheless he had to get some reward for his pains so he ordered all the passengers from the train. They were lined up along the track and robbed of whatever they had. In most cases this wasn't much. There were, however, some wealthy middle-class Mexicans travelling north to the States for business or pleasure and these were treated roughly, stripped of their belongings, and even their fine clothes, but otherwise unharmed. There were a few well-fed *gringos* and these Parra, personally, deprived of their fat wallets with a cheeky grin. 'You enjoy your stay in *Mexico*, huh?'

This reminded him of the two *gringos*, tied to the front of the locomotive. He led the way back to them. They appeared to be half-dead. He wondered what they had done to be described as bandits and murderers. He had his men cut them down.

'Aiiee! You guys.' He prodded them with the toe of his thigh-length boots as his men gave them water, fanned them with sombreros and tried to revive them. 'What you done that so bad, huh?'

Nathan tried to stumble to his feet, but collapsed forward revealing his flayed and festering back. 'Ai, yai! That is bad. Who did this to you?'

The water had brought Pete partly to his senses and he muttered,' Ramón Corral.'

'Corral! That bastard.'

'Yeah.' Pete's voice was slow and hoarse. 'You get me back to life — I'm going to kill him.'

'You're going to kill him?' Parra was a short, sharp-featured man, and he grinned at his first lieutenant, a burly individual, much broader about the face and girth. 'That's not a bad idea. How you gonna do that, *gringo*?'

'I'll catch up with him. Just get me and my *amigo* back to life.'

'Too bad, Yanqui,' Parra said, raising his revolver. 'We don't waste time with wounded.'

'Wait, Ignacio,' his lieutenant said, and stooped to pull away a paper pinned to the *gringo's* shirt. 'What's this?'

'Deportation order.' One of the bandits could read, with some difficulty. 'Pete Bowen, alias Pete Johnson, or Black Pete, for crimes against the state of Mexico, including murder of Colonel Ferdinand Veraco, and involvement in armed rebellion and treason in the state

64

of Sonora . . . to be handed over to the Texan authorities at the border post of El Paso.'

'You know, I heard about that.' Parra slapped the burly younger man on the shoulder. 'Veraco certainly deserved all he got. These guys fought alongside Cajeme and his Indians on the other side of the mountains. They took on Ramón Corral and his *federales* scum. Doroteo, get them into the shade.'

The lieutenant beamed as he dragged the two Texans into the shade beneath the train. 'Sounds like these two *hombres* should have a national monument erected in their honour.'

'*Si*, I officially pronounce them people's heroes.' Parra instructed his men to peel off their shirts and throw water over their suppurating backs. 'When we gain power I will have them sit in my cabinet.'

Doroteo grinned at Parra's political pretensions. 'When is that going to be, *jefe*?' He took a similar legal paper from the shirt of the blond Texan, and had it read to them. 'Nathan Strong. Former federal bureau investigator. Hmm!' he said. 'There's more to these two guys than meets the eye.'

A rough wagon had by this time arrived and Parra's wounded men were being loaded aboard. 'Put these two men on,' Doroteo ordered. 'Careful with them. Lay them face down. Take them to Maria's. That witch can bring anybody back from the dead.'

As the wagon rattled away Parra turned his attention to stripping the dead soldiers of their uniforms, weapons and ammunition. Maybe, he thought, the uniforms would come in useful once the revolution began.

★ ★ ★

Miguel came out of a coma in which he had sweated and dreamed strange dreams to find himself in the small jailhouse of San Juan. He was lying on a blanket on the hard floor and on the other side of the bars were two *rurales* playing cards with the village policeman.

'What happened?' he growled, thinking he might have been thrown in jail for being mad drunk. And he gasped as he tried to move: pain like a red-hot needle stabbed into his side. 'Aagh!'

The *rurales* laughed. 'Ah, so you live?' A greasy-faced fat one spat. 'I make a good *medico*, no? Dug His Excellency's slug out of you, myself. Cauterized it with gunpowder and my cigar. You owe me a life.'

Miguel examined what lay beneath the grubby, bloody bandage about his waist, expecting to see maggots. But, no, it did not look too bad. 'So, thanks. What you gonna do now, hang me?'

'You surely deserve it,' the fat one said. 'But no, Ramón Corral is merciful. His instruction is that if you live we invite you to join our ranks. You may become a *rurale*.'

'Huh!' Miguel tried to move. 'And if I refuse?'

The fat one flipped a card. 'We kill you.'

Miguel pondered this for a while. 'Why should Señor Corral make such an offer?'

'He has heard you are a man of considerable experience, a *vaquero*, a gunfighter, a hard man, one who has travelled far north of the border. You know America *del Norte*. Sometimes we have unofficial business there. You must understand that most of our recruits are from the prisons, rapists, murderers. They don't have a lot of juice in their coconuts. His excellency can use a man who knows his way around.'

'You can tell His Excellency to go stuff himself,' Miguel snorted. 'Why should I want to work for a butcher like him?'

The fat *rurale* roared with laughter again. 'Because you have no alternative. Hey, come on, the life is not so bad. You get as much rum as you can drink, meat three times a week, free use of

68

the army brothels. And a man can get rich.' He pointed to the silver *conchos* on his sombrero. 'How you think I get these?'

Miguel rubbed his dark-hued bald pate. 'Where are my friends?'

'Ah,' the village policeman said. 'You were fortunate not to have seen how they suffered, the *gringo* run, the flogging.'

'He was lucky not to have suffered it, too. Your two Yankee comrades will by now be languishing in prison in Texas.'

'What about our mine?'

'Ha! That is now the property of Señor Corral. As is the tall Texan's *señora*.'

'Louisa? What about Melody?'

'Pah! She is nothing. She has been sent to the brothels.'

'Looks like you sure sorted us all out.'

'Well, my friend, what is it to be? Are you with us?'

'Sure,' Miguel shrugged. 'What have I to lose?'

'There is no hurry,' the fat *rurale* said. 'When you are ready to get on a horse we will go join our regiment.'

★ ★ ★

Ramón Corral was banqueting in the governor's palace in San Luis Potosi when the telegraph was brought to him to tell him of the raid on the train to the north and the disappearance of the two *gringos*. His dark face seemed to drain of its colour for moments and then he stood up and exploded in anger, sweeping the plates from the table.

Louisa, sitting by his side, jumped like a startled racehorse as her low-cut dress was splattered with broken crockery and bits of food.

'What's the matter?'

'That damn *gringo* friend of yours. He's escaped.'

She drew herself up, pale and swan-necked in the diamonds Corral had insisted she wore. She smiled slightly fixing him with her dark eyes. 'So, Your Excellency? Are you afraid he might appear out of the dark one night to get you?'

Corral scowled at her, smashed his wine glass at a wall, and pointed a finger at the governor. 'This is your fault, Fernandez. I should have killed them, but you had to go tittle-tattling to *el presidente*.'

'Not at all.' Fernandez's lips twitched as he picked up his glass and took a sip of wine, as if nothing had happened. 'I was merely keeping our beloved Porfirio Diaz acquainted with the situation.'

'It is not too late,' Ramón Corral stormed, uncaring about the guests at the banquet. He snapped his fingers for his captain of guard. 'I want every available *rurale* to move out tomorrow. You go north to Chihuahua. I want the heads of these two Yankees and the bandit chief Parra. They are communists, renegades and rabble-rousers. They are a threat to the internal security of Mexico. They must be stopped.'

'Will Your Excellency be accompanying us?'

'No, I will return to Sonora.'

★ ★ ★

Bloody and haggard as the two Texans looked when they were cut from their bonds at the front of the train their injuries were not as bad as they appeared. That is, if a broken finger, bruised ribs, cuts and contusions to Pete's face, hands and chest could be regarded as 'not too bad'. Nathan had fared worse, his eye cut and inflamed from the kicks. Both had suffered from exposure to the burning sun by day, and the cold by night, their faces and lips cracked and burned. They would bear the marks of the whip on their backs for the rest of their days, and the scars on their souls. No man who had endured such a flogging was ever the same. But, under the care of the old 'witch', Maria, they survived. She made poultices of mountain herbs for their festering backs, and an odd-tasting tea for their insides. Like the Apache, who had once ravaged this northern state, she believed that the best treatment was fasting, rest, washing with clear water inside and out, and, of course, the incantation of magic charms.

Fittingly enough Maria's adobe house was outside a place called Jesus Maria, not far from the Lake de los Patos. It looked like any run-down hovel, a windpump, a tethered mule, bamboos, cactus, a crop of corn growing in the poor soil, but it had long been one of the main way-stations of the bandit Ignacio. One night there was the sound of horses' hooves clattering outside and his favourite lieutenant, Doroteo Arango, burst in.

'We got to be moving, *muchachos*,' he called. 'At this moment three hundred *rurales* are leaving the city of Chihuahua at the head of a battalion of soldiers. They are going to swoop through the *chapparal* leaving not a stone unturned. It is the biggest operation against us we have yet known.'

'Maybe that's our faults,' Nathan Stone said. 'Corral is bound to have put a price on our heads. Maybe we should head back to the States for a bit.'

'What, and leave the girls to their fate?' Pete stormed. 'I guess Corral might well be anxious if he knows we're loose.'

Nathan pursed his lips and studied the dust floor. 'I ain't sure there's a lot we can do. In my opinion them poor gals have already undergone their fate.'

'Come on, Nathan,' Pete urged. 'You ain't never let a little beating discourage you before.'

'What can we do? It's what the Frenchies call a *fait accompli*. You heard 'em. Melody's already in a brothel. And Louisa's Corral's wife.'

'That weren't a legal marriage and you know it. It was made under duress.

There ain't no way I'm goin' home just yet. An' who the heck taught you to speak French?'

The bandit, Doroteo, chubby-faced and broad of chest, produced a dead sucking pig from a sack on his side. The rest of the population of Chihuahua might be living in dire poverty, but bandits generally ate well. 'Life is brief,' he said. 'We eat, we drink, and then we ride.'

He went outside to see to the horses, and call in one of his companions. The other he stationed on the roof as a lookout. They were dressed much alike, in tight leather trousers, shabby jackets, and sombreros, bristling with crossed bandoliers of bullets, others around their waists, rifles and revolvers to hand. Doroteo was also wearing two wallets hanging over his solid belly, studded with cartridges. They were well-prepared for ambush and it was, in some ways, their symbol of, 'No quarter'. All in all they had a loud, swashbuckling air. Doroteo was already renowned for his bravery under fire that verged on the foolhardy. He scratched his curly hair and gave his odd-shaped grin, his hard-cut face speaking his ancestry, Spanish, Indian, and maybe a little Negro blood. Like most Mexicans he was a dark and mysterious mix. 'I bring you gifts,' he said, and produced from out of his deep wallets two revolvers.

'Whew!' Pete whistled with awe as he handled the long-barrelled revolver of high-polished blued steel. 'A Solingen. I heard of these. The same German company that makes the cutlery. Hey, ain't this the new swing-out cylinder?'

'Yes,' Nathan said. 'First time I've seen one. Makes for easier loading.'

Pete clacked it back and flicked it out again, peering along the flat-topped frame. He removed one of the cartridges. 'This, at least, has stopping power. 44 calibre. Ain't got no use for them puny .38s.'

He gripped the stock of chequered hard rubber. 'This is new, too. Probably stops the termites eatin' it. Well, Nathan, shall we toss for it?'

'It's yours, you old heathen. You're the boss. Guess I'll have to make do with this ole single action.' He picked up the other gun, a Colt Frontier .45, the notched walnut butt of which showed it had seen some action. He spun it on his finger and crouched aiming double-handed at the wall. 'Yeah, I think I *will* come with you.'

'I'm kinda used to one on each hip, but I guess with my finger broke this one's all I can use.' Pete licked his lips, hungrily, for Maria was busy at the big stone stove roasting the sucking pig over a bed of coals.

'Another present.' The bandit lieutenant pulled a bottle of what the Texans called dago red out of the capacious bag on his hip. 'Should put some fire back in you.'

'Hey!' Pete pulled the cork and took a deep swig, passing it to Doroteo. '*Salud*!'

'No. Me, I don' drink or smoke. But, you, go ahead.'

Nathan and the other Mexican took a pull as Maria began to carve the little pig to serve on wooden platters of chilli beans. It was a feast they had long been missing.

'How long you been riding with Parra?' Pete asked, for at close quarters in the candlelight Doroteo Arango appeared to have an open boyish face, if bulldog-like.

'Since I was thirteen. My family are peons on the great estate of Don Arturo Lopez Negrete. I was raised as a *charro*. You say cowboy.'

'Yep, I know the word.'

'We were virtual slaves. I ran away twice and got caught and flogged for my pains. The third time I met a *rurale* coming down a pass. I killed him with a rock to his head. I took his horse and gun and didn't go back.'

'You don't say. So, how old are you now?'

'Nineteen.'

'Yeah? Must be the moustache and the guns make you look older than your years.'

'Sometimes I think I was born old,' Doroteo said. 'I have seen much suffering. Ours is a backward country. Most of my people live at starvation level. Is there any wonder they have to drink the *pulque* to forget their woes. It is cheap enough. You just tap into a cactus. But it is not good. One day, maybe, we will give them something to live for, hope for.'

'Is that what Parra says?'

'It is what we both say. Before Diaz seized power we had a good man, an Indian, ruled this country, Benito Juarez. He divided the land among the poor, provided free schools and hospitals, freedom for the Press, abolished special privileges for the military and confiscated church property. He died in office in '72. Since then under Diaz, everything has gone to the dogs.'

'The dogs under Diaz at the top,

you mean? The politicians, the big landowners, the *rurales* and *federales*, the church: they sure know how to help themselves.'

'*And* the *gringos*.' Doroteo smiled, but his eyes were gem-hard. 'When we take power they will all have to go.'

★ ★ ★

They rode through the night beneath a full moon that bathed the high chapparal in its silver glow. They climbed up into the chasms of the great mountain chain, the Sierra Madre. Pete's injured ankle rested against the cold stock of a Marlin six-shot bolt action carbine tucked through the cinch of his mustang. It made him feel more in command of his destiny to be armed, to be back in the saddle, although he missed the power, the fingertip control of his black stallion. First, he figured, he would have to stay with these *bandidos*, fight the *rurales*, who had come looking for them. And then he would go looking for her. And woe betide anybody who tried to stop him. His whole body ached for vengeance.

5

They did not call Ignacio Parra 'The Puma' for nothing. He was as wild and as cunning, as fast and ruthless in attack, and as speedy in retreat as that lithe animal. He knew all the canyons and chasms of the western Sierra Madre carved by time by the tributaries that drained down to the distant Rio Conchos. But even he and his *bandidos* were hard put to escape the net thrown out across the land by the *rurale* horsemen, backed by hundreds of conscripted military. Parra, his men and the two *gringos* who rode with them, were harried from pillar to post, as the saying goes. They were pushed far north into the barren Journada de la Cardadero. They turned back and swept around their enemies' flank, passing close to their camps in the night. When they reached

Ojo Caliente they encountered another patrol. There was a pitched battle after which many of their own were left for dead. They fled up the Rio Carmen and escaped into the mountains.

There they were given shelter and sustenance by the people of Carmen. They crossed uncrossable crags and descended the Rio Sacramento riding into Sacramento to attack the military post behind the *rurales'* back. They grabbed what booty they could, fresh horses, food and ammunition, and fled up the Rio Nombre de Dios reaching the eyrie of Casachuichuachi where they rested up and licked their wounds.

The *rurales* and the military, however, had been ordered to carry out a war of attrition. They had learned their tactics well in Sonora on the other side of the mountains in their genocidal campaign against the Yaqui Indians. Once again they swooped on villages, questioned the peasants, who stood, in their white pyjama-like clothes, mute, straw hats in hands, saying nothing, knowing nothing of the bandits who had passed a few days before. In villages all across Chihuahua men who refused to speak were left hanging, the peons' meagre crops destroyed as a warning. The witch, Maria, was hoisted by her ankles and flogged to death. And even then she did not speak, and hardly cried out.

'It's a bad business.' Pete shook his head, sadly, as they cut her body down. 'So much pointless killing. Sometimes I'm tempted like you to get out of it, to head back to the States. This is a desperate land.'

'Yeah,' Nathan grunted as he began to dig a grave. 'She was a good old woman. But it makes you angry, too. One day somebody is going to have to pay.'

'You think we're riding on the right side?'

'Yeah, I think so. One day the whole damn country's going to rise up against Diaz, Corral and their ilk.'

'I don't know,' Pete sighed. 'I'm

anxious to get on the trail of Louisa and Melody. But these damn *bandidos* watch us like hawks.'

'There's no way we could get through to Durango or the south. There's military everywhere. You know that.'

'Maybe we could go back across the Sierra Madre into Sonora. It's my guess Corral has taken the girls back to his home state.'

'Maybe.' Nathan tied two sticks together as a cross and stuck it in the ground, taking off his hat to mutter a prayer. 'Maybe not. Mexico's a big country.'

'Hey, *amigos*.' Doroteo came to get them. 'We're moving out.' But he, too, crossed himself, and paused on one knee for a few moments beside the grave.

★ ★ ★

The Puma had had word from one of his spies that an American company was sending down a strongbox of greenback dollars to pay their employees working a silver mine in Durango. Instead of entrusting it to the railroad, which was regularly attacked by Parra, they were hoping to avoid trouble by using passenger stagecoach. Word was it was already on its way and heading for La Cruz on the Rio Conchos.

The *bandidos* rode hard for three nights and laid their ambush. On the fourth day they saw a pillar of dust and made out the stagecoach lumbering towards them, pulled by a six-horse team. They were not unduly surprised to see that it was well guarded by not only the shotgun guard but at least a dozen outriders. Parra grinned hyenalike through his grey-whiskered, narrow jaws, clacking back the bolt of his carbine. 'Ready, *muchachos*? Yankee dollars will be very useful to us.'

Pete wasn't too happy about attacking his own countrymen, because he could see what appeared to be a couple of Texans among the outriders. But the die was cast, so he climbed on to his horse, put the reins in his teeth, pulled his Marlin six-shot into his shoulder, kicked in his spurs, and went charging down from the rocks with the rest of them. Against forty wild, screaming, shooting *renegados* the outriders couldn't put up much of a fight. Pete and Nathan hardly needed to shoot. The shotgun and Mexican guards were toppled from their horses and the two Texans set off back the way they had come, whipping their horses for all they were worth.

Pete grinned as he watched them go. 'They ain't much of an advertisement for us men of the Lone Star State.'

Parra fired shots into the lock of the strong-box and whooped for joy as he examined the wads of brand-new greenbacks inside. There was nigh on ten thousand bucks. The grin of Pete, for one, was wiped from his face when he saw another plume of dust approaching from the direction the Texans had gone and heard the ground drumming to at least one hundred horses of a military patrol. They were splashing across the shallow river fast.

'Ignacio!' he shouted, and without hesitation aimed his carbine at the leading rider, saw him throw up his hands and tumble into the water. He drew the bolt and fired again. 'We gotta get outa here. Fast!'

But Ignacio Parra was struggling to get the strong-box roped to a mule. No way was he leaving without it. His men began scrambling on to their mustangs as lead whined and whistled about their heads. The *rurales* were coming at full tilt.

'Leave it!' Pete shouted, but Parra the Puma was not inclined to abandon his prey. He growled and struggled messily to tie the knots and hang on to the alarmed mule. Suddenly, as the unsteady box tumbled down, a bullet caught him in the jugular and blood gushed like a faucet from his neck. He stumbled and fell and within seconds the famed bandit leader was lying dead in the dust, his fingers still seeming to clutch for the strong-box.

Pete tossed his carbine and caught it by the barrel ready for hand-to-hand fighting. The sun was glinting on the *rurales'* sabres and, although they had taken some casualties, there was no way they were going to abandon their charge. When they hit all became desperate confusion, a whinnying of horses falling, screams of men decapitated and cut down by sabre slash, revolvers fired into faces, bandits leaping from horseback to grapple with the hated 'red capes', swinging daggers into chests, or dragging them to the ground and throttling them. Pete swung out with the carbine and heard a sombrero'd head crack apart like dry wood. He pulled it back and jabbed it into another's gut.

He fought his way to the edge of the fray, thrust the emptied carbine back beneath his leg, pulled the Solingen and fired at whatever grey-uniformed Mexican presented himself. As he spent his sixth slug and a bullet scorched his cheek, he whirled his mustang and looked about him. Outlaws lay dead and dying and the rest were hopelessly outnumbered. He caught Nathan's eye and waved him away. Doroteo Arango had the same idea, bellowing to his men to withdraw. He gave a regretful look back at his fallen chief and spurred his mount in a beeline for the hills, trailed by Pete, Nathan and a few survivors.

★ ★ ★

They were a mournful bunch of outlaws who tended their wounds that night. They brewed up coffee, looking down from the safety of their crags to the plain of the Rio Conchos and the scene of the battle. The *rurales*, the stagecoach and strong-box had gone on their way, taking the head of Ignacio Parra.

'Looks like you're in charge,' Pete said to Doroteo Arango, as they chewed on charred steaks of a horse that had broken its leg on the climb.

'Yeah.' Arango made a rueful face as he chewed. 'This damn hoss was as tough as the *jefe*.'

Pete eased out his long legs, leaned back on his saddle and tipped back his hat. 'Is that his obituary? Waal, he had a good run 'til his luck ran out. Wonder how much reward there was on his head.'

'*Muchos pesos*,' Arango said. 'Same as there is on me. Same as there is on you. We can have no rest. The *jefe's* bullet found him. Same as will mine. Same as will yours. It is the way of things. God decides.'

'Let's hope we've a while to go yet.'

'*Si*.' Arango gave a roar of laughter. 'You still think you got some living to do? Me, too.' He got up to piss in the thorns and go keep first watch.

★ ★ ★

'The average lifespan of a Mexican is thirty-six years,' Nathan drawled, as he rolled green-leafed tobacco in a corn husk. 'I was surprised when I first heard that. But I sure ain't since riding with these boys.'

'Thirty-six? That sounds kinda over-optimistic. If the rope, the bullet, the whip don't kill them, malnutrition does. That's a classy way of saying they starve to death.'

'It's a helluva country. What surprises me is they're still so damn cheerful.'

'A few swigs of that cactus juice will make anybody cheerful. I could do with a bottle of mescal right now to forget my woes.'

Nathan took a glowing twig of ocotillo from the fire and lit up, breathing out a billow of the noxious baccy.

'You keep smoking that you ain't gonna last long yourself.'

'How the hell we git into this, an' how the hell we gonna git out?'

They were lying beneath the midnight

stars when Arango returned and rolled up in his blanket by the fire, his carbine in his hand. 'OK, you Yanquis. Who goes next?'

'My turn I guess.' Nathan picked up his rifle and ambled away to the point of a crop of rocks to stand guard.

'Gimme a kick about four,' Pete said. He looked over at the Mexican. 'Where to *manaña*?'

'I got a bad feeling,' Arango said. 'I think I go home.'

'Me an' my buddy, we've been thinking. We got no objection to helping you boys fight your war, but we got personal business to attend to.'

'Oh, yeah?' Doroteo grunted, half asleep.

'Yeah. We gotta go find our wimmin. We figure Corral's taken 'em to Sonora. Any way we could get a guide to take us across those mountains?'

'Sonora? What you gonna do when you get there?'

'We'll sniff around. We want them back.'

For a while Pete thought that Arango had dozed off, for he had closed his eyes and had a benign smile on his face. Perhaps he was thinking of what he would do now he was the new *jefe*. He made a snorting, scoffing noise. 'You think you can beat *el gran general*?'

'Corral? Maybe.'

'Huh! OK. I give you a man to take you. Me I go down to Durango. Do a bit of rustling. Raise more men. If I let you go will you do something for me?'

'Such as?'

'There is a man. Francisco Madero. He is a lawyer, a man with much brains, you understand. He believes in our cause. Parra told me so. He is in exile in your country. If he came back Diaz would kill him. Madero has spoken out against him. He is high on the death list. I want you to go to see him. He is in a place called San Antonio. Will you bring him back?'

'Why?'

'I will make him president of Mexico.'

'You don't say?'

'Yes, I do say. There is a man called Emiliano Zapata in the south. There is a certain general in Sonora. They are dissatisfied with Diaz. I mean they want to kill him. If we all unite we can do this. We can chase him out of our country.'

'Hmm? Sounds like a mighty big if.' Pete yawned and tipped his hat over his eyes. 'OK. It's a deal. When I done what I gotta do I'll go get him.'

Doroteo leaned over and shook him. And when Pete opened one eye he saw he had his massive hand stuck out. He put up his own and gripped it.

'Me. You. We much alike,' the Mexican grinned. 'We got confidence. We believe in a better life. The future.'

'Yeah,' Pete said. 'It's a deal. To *mañana*.'

6

Ramón Corral, after a brief visit to his *hacienda* in Sonora, had taken his bride to Mexico City for he was to be installed as vice-president of the country, and he wished to combine the occasion with a grandiose wedding ceremony. Perhaps the nuptials in San Juan had been a farce, but this would be the real thing so that no man could challenge him as to its legality.

Louisa was decked in a glittering wedding dress which had cost thousands of *pesos*, and required a dozen page-boys to carry her train as she progressed down the aisle of the magnificent cathedral in the city's main square, the Zócalo. Anyone of importance had been invited to attend. Louisa was tempted to tear off her veil and cry out that she had been taken against her will, but one look at her surly bemedalled groom awaiting her at the altar told her this was not a good idea. Instead she murmured her responses, and when the organ music crashed out she knew that she was truly married. She even managed to smile as she left the church on her husband's arm.

Ramón's threats as to what would happen to her if she did not behave, and what he would do to the *gringos*, had sunk deep into her psyche. In public he, and his fawning courtiers, treated her like a grand lady. It had been announced in the *periodicos* that she was of ancient Spanish aristocracy, and, indeed, she was. What was not revealed was that she was the bastard child of her mother and a groom who worked in the stables. Louisa's birth had been hushed up and she had never seen her mother since. She believed her to be living somewhere in the USA. Louisa had been brought up for a while by the nuns and returned to her father when she reached her teens. She lived among the peons in her village until the ancient Don Ignacio decided he wanted her. The Texan, Pete, saved her from that fate after her father had been flogged to death in an attempt to protect her. Now, it seemed, his sacrifice had been in vain. Her destiny was to be the bullying Corral's wife and plaything.

From being an innocent village girl, and for one wonderful year the wife of an easy-going Texan mine-owner, she was now hemmed about by the constraints of Mexican society. Her life seemed to consist of changing dresses, or being dressed by her maids, one dress for breakfast, another for luncheon, and yet another for dinner. How many dresses did a girl need? It was an enervating round of parties, balls, introductions, but only to those high on the social scale. She was never allowed to be familiar with ordinary people, or leave the confines of her grand homes.

For his induction as vice-president Ramón wanted her to look even more dazzling than she had done on their wedding day for it was to be an important occasion with numerous statesmen from other countries in attendance, Great Britain, Germany, the United States, even the newly modernized Japan. For fear these dignitaries might set eyes on them Corral ordered all the beggars and 'shoeless', any Indian or peasant who might offend the eye, and there were plenty of them, to be swept from the main streets of the capital back to the slums where they belonged.

Louisa, herself, could not deny she was dazzled by the opulence of the investiture and the banquet on solid gold plate of innumerable courses afterwards. When she heard the US ambassador describe Diaz as 'one of the great leaders of mankind who has brought his country out of darkness into the sun' and her husband as 'a lover of justice and liberty' she began to wonder if there might not be some truth in this. Why otherwise would all these notable people join in such eulogies?

There was a press conference afterwards at which Diaz and Corral answered carefully vetted questions by foreign and national journalists. One youngish editor of a Mexico City paper, Lucas Guttierriez, took the opportunity to pour out his anger. Was it true, he asked, that ten million in US dollars had vanished into contractors' pockets for a thousand miles of supposedly completed railroad track which he could prove was non-existent?

Before the off-guard Ramón could hush him up he had let fly a string of accusations. What of the plight of the Yaqui Indians, the villages burned, the massacre ordered by Corral in which *rurales* buried their victims standing in a field and rode over their heads? What of the bribery of the judiciary? What of the generals who ran gaming houses and brothels and collected pay for regiments where they had no more than platoons? He pointed a finger to indict Corral, but didn't get much further before he was hustled away.

While Ramón stormed and denied these 'allegations of a lunatic', the benign, white-haired half-Indian, Diaz, smiled and informed them that the new electrical chair was to be used for the execution of criminals . . . wasn't that progress? In other words, he implied — Beware!

That night the new vice-president staggered drunkenly into Louisa's chamber. When she asked him what had happened to Guttierrez, he snarled, 'He got what he deserved, that gutter scribbler.'

'He only wished to speak the truth.'

Corral laughed at her and told her he had better things for her to do with her pretty mouth than talk bilge. It was not unusual for him to force her into degrading acts that she imagined were fit only for some slut in a brothel. Afterwards, Corral's hairy chest reverberated as he snored like a pig. Once again Louisa reached to carefully take his revolver. She knelt over him, wishing she had the courage to put a pillow over his head and blow him away. Ramón's eyes opened and for seconds he regarded her, seriously. Then he snatched the revolver from her and tossed it aside. 'You haven't got the guts.' He rolled on top of her again. 'You love the way I treat you, my lady,' he grinned. 'You pretend you don't, but you do.'

She was sitting at breakfast the next morning, when Ramón grunted, 'You want to see Lucas Guttierrez. Come! I take you to him.'

In their closed coach they drove to the barracks of the *federales* with its adjoining prison for *politicos*. Louisa's heart filled with dread as doors clanged and they descended into dark, dank cellars, a jailer leading the way. A cell door was unlocked and in the light of a tar flare she saw a half-naked man lying on the floor. His body and face were lacerated by wounds. She could hardly recognize Guttierrez.

The young newspaperman blinked

at them and managed to say through swollen lips, 'Get me a lawyer . . . I must have a lawyer.'

'Don' worry,' Corral laughed. 'You'll get a fair trial, in a year or two.'

He suddenly grabbed Louisa by the hair at her nape and thrust her down at him. 'Take a good look. This is what happens to those who speak treason.'

He pulled her up and slammed her against the wall. 'You got to make up your mind once and for all time, Louisa. You want me to leave you with him? Or you want to be loyal to your husband in your nice comfortable mansion? You can only have it one way.'

Louisa glanced wildly at Guttierrez, at what appeared to be an open sewer in the corner of the room, and tensed as she saw a rat slithering along the drain. 'Take me home,' she whispered, huskily.

★ ★ ★

Doroteo Arango led the two *gringos*, and what remained of his band, a dozen scarred and weary *bandidos*, towards a village nestled in the foothills. It was little different to countless other villages scattered about the arid northern plateau region of Chihuahua. A few adobe houses at the crossroads of rutted tracks; chickens, skinny pigs, pariah dogs scampered out of the way of their horses' hooves. A silence hung over the place, a sleepy silence of a way of life unchanged by modern times.

'This is my home,' Arango called. 'This is where I was born.' He reined in beside one of the houses set back beside a stone-walled corral. 'This is my mother's house.'

He called out but nobody came out to the forecourt to greet him. He stepped down with a puzzled look. 'Maybe somebody has died?'

Pete decided to stretch his legs too, and see if there was a chance of something cool to drink. He looked through the portal of the main living-room and saw a youth, younger and slighter than Doroteo, but with the same stamp of features. Instead of responding to Doroteo's jovial hug his face remained solemn. He whispered something and nodded to a pile of blankets that served as a bed. An air of mourning hung over the house.

Pete followed them in and saw a dark-haired peasant girl huddled on the bed, quietly sobbing. An old woman, her mother, stroked at her hair. Doroteo went down on one knee and kissed her hand. 'Mama, what has happened?' he asked.

The old woman, her head covered by her shawl, hardly deigned to notice him. 'You come back now when it is too late,' she muttered.

'What do you think has happened?' the young man spat out, bitterly. 'While you are away riding with your bandit friends what do you know of what we have to bear?'

'Don Arturo Negrete?' The bandit

leader spun on him, gripped his arms. 'Tell me, was it he?'

'His son, Leonardo.'

'Leonardo?' Again Arango appeared puzzled. 'He is the same age as me, I have known him since a boy. Why didn't you stop him?'

'Ha! Stop him? Stop him and his *charros*? That is easy to say. Anyway, I was out in the fields. Since Father died I have to look after us on my own. Do you think I, too, wouldn't like to run away?'

Arango's face had puffed up with anger, his dark eyes bulging. He pushed his brother away and placed his hand on his sister's shoulder. 'When did this happen?'

'Early this morning,' the brother said. 'They came to the house.'

'I, Doroteo, will avenge this wrong they have done to you, to my family,' Arango hissed.

The girl looked up, her face streaked with tears, and screamed, 'No!'

Arango spun on his heel, his spurs

jingling, and strode out. His brother ran after him. 'Don't do this, Doroteo. Please, leave it be. You will only bring more trouble.'

'Mount up,' Arango shouted. '*Arriba, gringo!* We go!'

They went spurring out of the village on their fiery mustangs, leaving the brother staring after them. They headed straight as an arrow across the dusty plain. 'Where are we going?' Pete shouted.

'To the hacienda of Leonardo Negrete, son of Don Arturo Lopez Negrete, the rancher who owns this estate.'

'You sure this is a good idea?'

'My family, these people, they are serfs. They have no rights. But we, too, are human. Sometimes the *haciendados* go too far.'

Pete had heard of the estate owners exercising their seignurial rights over virgins, taking a girl against her will, and handing her on to whoever might be her prospective husband. Generally, it was mutely accepted. Like the boy said, what could they do against armed *charros*? But, hadn't he himself stepped in on behalf of Louisa? He understood how Arango felt. And not every ex-virgin had a bandit for a brother who was as angry as a bull.

When they sighted the walled gateway, with its lookout on the rampart, which guarded the *hacienda* of Don Arturo's son, Arango did not hesitate. He raised his rifle on saddleback and sent the guard spinning. Two men who ran to close the gates received the same treatment. Arango and his small band of guerillas went charging on.

If all the *charros* kept on the estate had been about the ranch they would have had no chance. But, fortunately for them, most of the cowboys were out about their business on the range. Only a few of Leonardo's cronies were lounging about the corrals and courtyard, not expecting trouble, and enjoying a half-dozing siesta in the hot sun. When they heard the shots they scrambled to their feet, but by then it was too late. The *bandidos* came swirling in on a cloud of dust, firing in every direction. Pete gritted his teeth and took out three *vaqueros* with successive shots, his revolver held at arm's length. The Solingen barked again and two more Mexicans were bowled over like jack-rabbits.

When the last five bodyguards backed away into the house and continued firing from the windows, Arango took cover and called out to them to surrender.

'What do you want?' one shouted.

'I want Leonardo,' Arango yelled. 'Or do you want us to burn this place down about you?'

There were a few moments silence. The great oak main door opened, and Leonardo Negrete stepped out. He was young, black-haired and handsome, and dressed in an open-necked ruffled shirt of white linen, a jacket threaded with gold like a bullfighter's, and tight velvet trousers. He had an arrogant jut to his head, for never before in his life had anyone attacked or even questioned his authority, and there was a sneer to the cut of his shaven jaws. 'I would strongly advise you men to go away before my father hears of this!'

Arango gave a scoffing growl of laughter. 'You would, would you? Don't you remember me, young *señor*?'

'Yes, you are Doroteo Arango. Bandit scum.'

'This morning you raped my sister. I have come for vengeance.'

Leonardo's face blanched. 'She was willing,' he shouted out, as he began to back away into the house. 'I assure you.'

'So you add insult to injury?'

Leonardo had a rifle in his hand and he jerked it wildly upwards. But, he was too late. A lariat landed over his shoulders and one of the mounted *bandidos* dragged him forward into the dust.

'You men in there,' Arango grinned, as a knife was put to Leonardo's throat. 'We got your boss. You better come out. Throw away your guns first.'

Pete was reloading his revolver and glanced uneasily, at Nathan. The *charros*, however, were not shot down as they gave themselves up. They were trussed and tied to the hitching rail.

'I want you to watch. I want you to let people know what happens to anyone who touches a hair of the head of any of the Arango family. One day, let them be warned, I would hunt them down and they would get worse than this.'

'What are you going to do?' Leonardo pleaded, as he got to his feet. 'Please, no!' He clutched at Arango's boot. 'My father will pay you a fortune in ransom.'

Doroteo gripped him by his grape-black hair and spat in his face. He tossed him away. 'Crucify him!'

Two of his *bandidos* dragged Leonardo to back up against the big oak door. There was an uneasy break as others went off to search for nails. Leonardo was trembling uncontrollably

111

and had to be supported by the men. 'No,' he repeated. 'No.'

'Come on, Arango,' Pete snapped out. 'Why not just shoot him and get it over.'

'You keep out of this,' Arango grunted. 'A bullet is too good for this swine. Good, here they come.'

The men's faces were dark and harsh as they hammered six-inch nails into Leonardo's palms, thighs and feet, as others held him, ignoring his frantic writhing, his screams.

'Hand over your revolver, *amigo*,' one of the mounted men said, jabbing his own into Pete's side. 'I don't trust you. You got an itchy finger.'

Pete reluctantly parted with his Solingen and Nathan was likewise deprived of his Colt. Arango grinned at them viciously as he jumped from his horse, and strode over to the youth. 'Now you see Mexican justice. Now you see the vengeance of Doroteo Arango against all landowners. You see what is to come.'

He reached for a pointed iron bar his men had brought from the carpentry shop and stared into Leonardo's tormented eyes. 'This is for my sister. Die!' He tensed his powerful shoulder muscles and thrust the spike deep into the youth's side. He pulled it out dripping blood, and tore it into the other side.

'Jesus!' Pete said, swallowing his disgust.

'Yes, just like He died. But this one will not rise again.' He drew the spike behind his head and plunged it into Leonardo's heart.

Arango stood breathing heavily, staring at the writhing, dying youth. He left the iron bar jutting from chest, and turned away, picking up his sombrero. He swung on to his horse and, without bothering to search for booty, led his men at a canter through the sprawled bodies of men fixated in death. Out through the gateway they rode, out at a steady lope towards the hills.

7

True to his word Arango found a villager who would lead Pete and Nathan across the mountains. '*Mi buen amigo*, Carlos,' he said hugging the old man. 'Don't forget, we meet in Durango.'

'God willing,' Pete muttered.

He and Nathan both spoke Texan Spanish, but sometimes they found it difficult to comprehend Mexicans.

'*Este caballo es mio*,' Carlos said, taking hold of the bridle of Pete's mustang.

'What's he saying?'

Arango guffawed, gruffly. 'He want it as payment for taking you.'

'What am I going to ride?'

'You're not. A horse will never make it over those peaks. You will have to buy or steal one the other side.'

'In that case he might as well have

114

mine.' Nathan offered his reins to him.

The grizzled old peasant shook his head. '*Nada.*'

'One horse is his price. No more,' Arango, said. 'We'll take the other.'

As they climbed up into the great crags Pete saw the impossibility of getting horses across. It hardly seemed possible for a man to climb up that sheer wall that hung over them. The peon had insisted they take off their narrow-toed, high-heeled boots and put on *huraches*, cheap, rope-soled sandals. As they scrambled up through the sharp boulders and scrub they saw the sense in this. Slowly, steadily, they left the foothills of the high plateau behind them and approached the great wall of rock. Beyond it they could see the tips of snow-capped pinnacles.

'Hail,' Nathan moaned, as they rested for a breather and looked back at Chihuahua stretched out beneath them. 'I sure hate being outa the saddle. It don't feel right.'

'Come on, cowboy,' Pete grinned. 'We only just started.'

They had brought a minimum of baggage; a rifle, wrapped by a blanket and macinaw, roped across their backs; belt of cartridges; a sack strapped across a shoulder containing a few essentials, flour, matches, tough red sausage the locals chewed, if they were in funds. They had a canteen of water on their belt and their boots strung around their necks. They camped the first night under a boulder, kept their fire low. The old man puffed on a *cigarillo* rolled in coarse brown paper, said little, staring into his own thoughts. Not that Pete or Nathan wanted to talk much. Their bodies ached too much from the unaccustomed climbing. They moved out before dawn.

The arid plateau of Chihuahua had, itself, an average height of 6,000 feet, so by late afternoon they had climbed to an altitude of some 8,000 feet, left the cactus and scrub, and entered a dark sinister belt of spruce and fir.

It was like entering a different life zone. They caught sight of chickadees and spotted flycatchers flitting through the branches, the same bird life they had seen further north in the States. At least there was plenty of wood for their fire that night. The only trouble was they couldn't get much sleep for the screeching of owls. At dawn Pete shot a brace of band-tailed pigeons. They plucked and roasted them for breakfast.

'Ain't seen a durn soul,' Nathan marvelled, sucking on a mug of hot black coffee. 'But them buzzards spiralling up there sure got their beady eyes on us. Mebbe they figure us for their next breakfast.'

Soon they had left the treeline far below, climbing single file after their guide, who seemed to know the way instinctively for there was not the faintest sign of even a goat track. He zigzagged back and forth, digging fingers and toes into crevices in the rocks, hauling himself up sheer faces if he could not find a way round. He tossed a rope down to the two cowboys and helped them make the ascent.

'Jeez,' Nathan shouted, as he swung suspended in space, his feet flailing. 'I hope these gals appreciate what we're doing for 'em.'

Maybe it was meant as a joke, but Pete's gaunt, bearded face took on a melancholy look that night as he crouched staring into the fire, his blanket wrapped around his shoulders against the chill, never-ceasing wind. Maybe it was all a wild goose chase? What odds were there against them ever finding Louisa and Melody, let alone rescuing them? For the first time he began to feel his age. What was a man of more than forty doing climbing over the central spine of Mexico?

It was a long, exhausting haul, trudging after Carlos, keeping their eyes on his bronzed shins as he scrambled up above them. Soon they entered fields of ice and snow, the Tierra Fria, and Pete figured they must be near 9,000 feet up. Nathan complained of dizziness and nose bleeds.

'Yeah, I knew a gal who suffered from that when I was a marshal up in Nevada,' Pete mused. 'Mountain sickness. It killed her. She fell a thousand feet down a precipice. You all right, boy? Maybe we should rope ourselves together?'

'Yeah, I'm OK now I know what it is. If it's only the altitude we'll soon be out of it. I thought maybe I'd picked up some kind of fever.'

'No, it ain't catching. Come on, cowboy. We gotta keep up with Carlos. He's way ahead.'

But, they weren't soon to be out of it. First another, and yet another mountain ridge reared up before them. They spent nights huddled down, shivering, without a fire for there was no wood for fuel. They had entered the bleak icy realm of the condor and twice they saw that great bird, like a creature from pre-history, floating and spiralling effortlessly out in the space all about them.

'You sure you know the way?' Pete asked, blowing on his gloved hands, beginning to worry about frostbite to their sandalled feet. He put socks and boots on again, but it didn't make walking easy.

Carlos's grey eyes glimmered with amusement through their puckered lids. '*Gringos* crazy!'

'Yeah, maybe you got a point. OK, let's move. Sooner we're through these mountains the happier I'll be.'

Both men began to wonder secretly if they ever would get through, if this Mexican wasn't leading them to their deaths, as they battled on after him through a damp grey mist of cloud. But, no! Could it be possible? On the crest of a high ridge they paused, and suddenly the clouds parted, and the sun's rays gleamed on the slopes leading down to the western plain of Sonora and the Pacific Ocean in the far distance.

'You go,' Carlos said, and pointed to a valley which appeared passable. 'You OK.' He shook hands with them and turned to go back to his village. '*Vaya con Dios*,' he called.

'Yeah, I guess we might need His help.' Pete led the way scrambling and sliding down, ploughing on his bootheels through a scree of loose shale uncaring that he might break a leg. Maybe it was the altitude, or the lack of food and sleep, but he felt elated as he went skiing down. 'Yee-haaugh!' he screamed.

When they reached the foothills Nathan shot a mountain goat and they feasted on the tough and scraggy beast. It seemed a shame to leave a good part of him behind, but at least the ravens would eat. 'All we gotta do now is buy ourselves some hosses, or a mule, or whatever we can get, and head for Sonora City.' Both men had silver in their belts from banditry.

'Yeah,' Nathan mused. 'Huccome you allus make it sound so easy?'

8

Life as a *rurale* had its advantages as far as Miguel was concerned. The pay was good, he ate and drank well, and he was provided with a fine horse and as much ammunition as he could use. He had no love for Ramón Corral or President Diaz, but he guessed as long as he was taking the president's peso he had to prove himself. He had always been a soldier of fortune, and, although contemptuous of most set in authority, he had worked as a lawman alongside Pete Bowen in Dodge City and Abilene. He had also ridden with him as an outlaw. He had seen much bloodshed in his day, and Mexico was a land bathed in blood. So he hardened himself and rode with the *rurales* through Durango and Zacatecas seeking out all those who gave refuge to the bandit Arango, or supported the rebellious doctrines of Francisco Madero, who had set himself up in opposition to Ramón Corral. Miguel did not like it, but he winced, and got on with the job when ordered to string up half-a-dozen Madero-istas, or put a man up against a wall and shoot him for speaking treason against *el presidente*. Why did the fools have to wear their hearts on their sleeves? If that was how they felt why didn't they take to the hills and join Arango?

Miguel didn't have much time for the little Creole, Madero, son of a rich *haciendado*, who had attended Jesuit college in Mexico and completed his studies in Paris and California. His head was filled with some funny ideas. He was known as 'the chocolate fool' for his habit of giving his large allowance away to the poor.

Madero had written a book sensationally attacking the policies of President Diaz and calling for free and fair elections. Ramón Corral had replied by sending in his *rurales* to break up Madero's meetings. But the five foot two inch 'fighting cock' had persisted with his demands. So much so that Corral had had him arrested on a trumped-up charge and put in jail in San Luis Potosi until elections were safely over. When he was released on bail Madero fled to the United States, but he still continued to stir up trouble from *el norte*.

'So, *amigo*,' the fat sergeant asked him. 'What do you think of the crazy Madero?'

'He's got guts.' Miguel shrugged, for he had a deep distrust for all politicians. 'But nothing will change whoever gets in. It's all pie in the sky.'

'Nonetheless, the man is dangerous. We should never have let him get away. There is a lot of support for him among the ordinary peons.'

'Ha! Maybe, but who is going to lead them? The bandit Arango? Or will the little man come back at the head of his own army to spout his platitudes?'

Their company had been ordered north-west to Sonora. They had taken the new railroad from San Luis Potosi up along the narrow coastal plain through the state of Sinaloa, on and on, further and further north until they reached the start of the Sonoran plain at Hermasillo.

As he sat among his noisy, drunken comrades and watched the plain unfold Miguel pondered on the strange fate that had brought him to be one of these hated and feared killers. But he was a man who accepted whatever throw of life's foolish dice. It was better than being dead. Up here the battle against the Yaqui indians had been more or less won, and they might get a break from executing fools for 'treason'. Life was cheap in Mexico, whatever side a man rode on.

'I've been keeping an eye on you,' the fat sergeant was saying as they rattled along on the railroad. 'I guess you know that. I thought at first you might be squeamish about joining us. But you've performed your duties like a true patriot.'

'Yeah?' Miguel's eyes glinted in his strong, sun-darkened face. 'I pass muster, huh?'

'*Si*. I have informed the vice-president of this. He wants to meet you. Tomorrow we will ride out to his *hacienda*.'

'Yeah?' Miguel adjusted for comfort the hunting knife in the sash of his tight, grey, embroidered uniform, and hitched up his gunbelt as they drew into their destination. 'What's he want to see me for?'

'You will find out.'

★ ★ ★

Miguel was kept busy as his company moved into the barracks in Hermasillo, arranging his kit by his bunk, cleaning his rifle, seeing to his horse.

'So, *amigo*,' the fat sergeant said, after they had filled their bellies with roast kid and wine, 'how about we go try the women?'

'That proposition is one I have never

refused.' Miguel flashed a grin. 'Where do we find them?'

'Follow me.' The sergeant had shaved and was liberally splashing perfume about his cheeks, oiling back his hair, giving a polish to his boots. 'Everything is laid on for us *rurales*. We have a fine life, ha?'

'I ain't raising no objections,' Miguel said, as they strode out, spurs clattering, into the town. Dinners, such as they were, had been slowly partaken, and the respectable class of the city, the shop-owners, lawyers, small businessmen, and their families were taking part in the nightly *paseo*. This involved strolling slowly around the *plaza* in one direction, while another stream moved anti-clockwise. Gentlemen would raise their hats and pause to chat, *señoritas*, watched by their chaperones, would flurry their fans and give secretive smiles as groups of eligible, or ineligible, young men stopped and sang compliments, hopefully. Idlers in the open-air cafés under the colonnades would be inclined to make much more ribald comments, while on a bandstand in the centre a military ensemble played poorly. Those of the lower class, and there were many, boot-blacks, beggars, purveyors of spicy snacks, would hawk their wares persistently, while the less fortunate or hopeless would lie asleep on benches or in doorways. Whoever they were they quickly made room when they saw two *rurales* swaggering towards them.

They had a couple of beers in a *cantina* and the sergeant led Miguel along a shady side street to the back of the shops. There they found a cobbled lane that was guarded by a military sentry-box at its entrance. The sergeant touched his sombrero to the guards and they walked through.

Down a steep hill they went. There were small shops on either side lit by oil flares. Outside each were groups of noisy *rurales* and *federales* and Miguel soon saw that the wares on display inside were women and girls. There were bars on the windows to cage them in like animals. Some stood gesticulating at their tormentors, or beckoning them inside. Some of the women were vastly bosomed, hirsute and horrendously ugly, and, funnily enough, these seemed to be the most popular because they gave the best show to the jeering men. One such poor creature rushed at the onlookers, turned, pulled up her skirts and presented a vast bare backside. Most appeared to be slightly demented.

'They are not free, but they are pretty cheap, eh?' the sergeant said, pushing Miguel forward and pointing to a card in a window offering services for a few pesos. The men, like most men who frequented such streets of shame, were mostly gawping in a hangdog manner, or haggling over the price. Not all were eager to enter these female dens.

Miguel grinned as he saw a *rurale* venture through one glass-fronted doorway and be grabbed by two of the inmates, who fought to drag their prey away into a covered booth like two black spiders. At the same time, unconcerned, another of the prostitutes skimpily clad, pushed out with a tray to go buy her friends cakes from the street's eatery.

Miguel and the fat sergeant pushed on through the throng down the little cul-de-sac until they reached the dark end where business was slow and the women more desperate. Indeed, one hook-nosed woman in nothing but a corset ran out, grappled with the sergeant and dragged him into her shop. He waved, like a gesticulating swimmer giving up the struggle, grinning foolishly as he was pulled behind a curtain.

Miguel lit a cheroot and waited, watching the antics of the girls. Some were skinny little things, not much older than fifteen. He wondered how they had managed to get thrown into such a hole. Maybe they didn't have much say in the matter, or got time off a prison sentence for serving here? One of them, a rather plain, gawky young woman, in a chemise and little else, was sitting on a chair, spectacles on her nose, seriously knitting a woollen vest, oblivious to it all.

The sergeant eventually re-emerged, all smiles, his treble chins wobbling as he straightened his uniform, and detailed what had occurred. 'Very enjoyable, *amigo*. Aren't you going to try?'

'I don't know.' Miguel gave his husky growl. 'I ain't seen one I'm particularly attracted to.'

The truth was, although he had no aversion to normal rowdy bordellos of the Mexican kind, he found this street profoundly depressing. It gave off the dank, hopeless air of some dilapidated zoo.

They were progressing back up the lane when he paused to look in another window. 'The usual clutch of pathetic half-wits,' he muttered to himself. And then his heart seemed to turn to stone. At the back of the crowd of women was a dark-haired, brown-complexioned young one with a more healthy look than most. She was dressed simply in a man's white shirt, which revealed her shapely legs, unbuttoned at the top to give a hint of the ripeness of her breasts. There was a solemn, haunted look in her eyes, but she coolly went through the motions of bartering. She caught Miguel's intent look beneath his sombrero and pointed to the sign on the window, signifying with the flat of her palm to ignore this, and pointing to eight fingers. She was cutting her price from, say, twenty-five cents to twenty.

The girl, whose full cheeks had once been beautiful, but now looked ravaged, knitted her brow with the flicker of a questioning look. Miguel tipped his hat to hang on his uniformed back and reveal his sunburned dome. He saw her red lips open with surprise. It was Melody.

'I'm gonna have one of these dames,' he said. 'I'll see you along at the *cantina*.'

The sergeant slapped him on the shoulder. 'Have fun, *hombre*.'

Miguel edged into the brightly lit cage, easing through the half-naked women until he reached her. 'Hi,' he breathed, as she gripped his hands, eagerly, and drew him into a cubicle.

There was a simple cot on to which they sank, Melody hanging on to him as he hugged her. He could feel her body trembling with emotion. 'It's so good to see you,' she said. 'I thought you were dead. But what are you doing here? Why are you dressed like this?'

Miguel held her at arm's length and studied her. 'I'm a *rurale*. It was the only option.'

'A *rurale*? But you, we . . . we hate them. Have you any news of Nathan? Of Pete?'

'No, 'cept the *periodico* said they were captured by Doroteo Arango. I figure those boys will be still alive.'

'Thank God. Thank Our Lady of Guadaloupe who I have been praying to.'

'Hey, you two! What you hangin' about for?' A woman put her head through the curtain partition. 'If you don't want her, soldier, you can have me.'

Melody glanced at him, shyly, although she had almost forgotten what modesty was in this place. 'Perhaps,' she said, 'perhaps we should pretend to be — so we can talk.'

'Suits me.' He grinned at her and rolled her over beneath him on the dirty straw palliasse. 'It feels funny to have my *amigo's amour* in my arms. How you like it in here?'

'How can you ask? It is horrible. All these men like filthy sweating apes. It is so good to see a friend.'

'Yeah?' Miguel stroked her face and studied her. 'But you were seeking my custom just now before you knew it was me.'

'I have to in order to eat. Any extra pesos we use for drinks and treats. It is this or — '

Miguel made a croaking sound, passing a thumb across his throat. 'How long they give you?'

'Twenty-five years . . . twenty-five years in this place. I will be an old woman by the time I get out. If I ever do, if I don't die of some botched abortion or the pox.'

'Come on, Melody. It ain't so bad. You're lucky to be alive. You killed old Don Ignacio, didn't you? If you were a man you would have been hanged.'

'Lucky? You call this lucky? So many times I have wished to be dead. Could you live like this?'

'Well, no. I am a man. But a woman, she is the passive one. It is not so bad.'

'I can't believe you are saying that, Miguel. We are friends. We rode free together. We went through fire. We fought these people. You have got to help me get out of here. You must.'

'Mmm?' At that moment Miguel was aroused by the warmth of her fulsome breasts pressed against him, and suddenly more interested in getting into her. 'I'll work on it.'

'No!' she protested, as his hands

squeezed and moulded her, and his mouth sought her lips. 'No! Not you!'

'Come on,' he coaxed. 'You must know I always wanted you. Same as you wanted me.'

'No! Miguel. It's not right. I thought you — '

But Miguel was never a man to be argued with. He was ripping his clothes off to reveal a body as hard and as muscled as a mustang's and as eager. He manhandled her into position, smothering her protest with his mouth, brooking no dissent.

Melody closed her eyes, clinging to him, and cried out, 'Oh, my God!'

'There!' Miguel flashed a gold-toothed grin at her some time later, feeling a morsel contrite when he came to his senses. 'That wasn't so bad. Old Nathan was a lucky guy.'

'Lucky?' Why do you go on about lucky? All you think of are your own lusts. What about Louisa? Is it right Corral has taken her as his wife?'

'Yeah, hear tell. Here.' He pressed

136

some silver pesos into her hand as he buttoned up his embroidered grey uniform. 'I must pay my dues like all the rest.'

'You think Pete will go after her?'

'I don't know. He's crazy enough for anything.'

'Miguel.' She put her arms around his strong neck and gave him a sad-sweet smile. 'If you get me out of here I can be *your* woman. I promise you.'

He unhooked her hands and threw her away. 'How can I do that? This place is more strongly guarded than a prison. I've seen the big iron gates at the end of the street. You think I'm going to throw away what I've got? A *rurale*'s is not a bad life.'

'*Rurale!*' Her face was contorted as she stared at him. 'Those scum. Those murderers. Is that all you think of friendship? How can you?'

'Yeah?' He hitched tight the stout leather belt around his waist, shoved his Paterson revolver into it. 'You think I'm a turncoat? Well, I tell you girl, yes, we rode together. But the sun sets, the world turns, there is another day. All that is past. I have to follow my chances.'

'Your chances?'

'*Si*. I laboured like a mule down a silver mine for a year for Señor Pete Bowen. What did I get out of it? I have a sixth sense of danger. That day, I told him we should go. But he wouldn't listen to me. Nor would you. Sure we were friends. Where, I would like to know, are the profits from that mine? In some Texan bank account? They are not in mine.'

'You know Pete wouldn't cheat us. That money was for all of us. To buy a ranch.'

'Yeah, well, maybe. But I'm tired of maybe. Today I ride on the winning side. I plan on getting rich, on buying my own *rancho* here in Mexico. And I can do that by working for Ramón Corral. I am tired of always fighting for promises.'

She sat abjectly on her cot, her

knees pressed together, her head bowed. 'Corral,' she whispered. 'you are one of his. I never thought to hear this.'

'A man has to swim with the tide. He can't be forever fighting it. Diaz and Corral rule this country. If I serve them life could be sweet.'

'Miguel, please.' There were tears trickling from her eyes, runnelling down her cheeks. 'Help me. I don't think I can stand it here much longer.'

'Aw, come on,' he said, awkwardly consoling her. 'Things ain't so bad. You know, maybe that ain't a bad idea, you being my woman. Maybe I can bargain with Corral. He wants me to do something for him. My services for your freedom, huh?'

Melody blinked through her tears, trying to smile up at him. 'You get me out of here I would be yours, Miguel.'

'Hang on in, gal. I'm not quitting on you.' Miguel pulled back the curtain and stepped out among the whores. '*Adios*, honey,' he shouted, smiling lecherously. 'And thanks. That was *muy bien*.'

* * *

In the morning they rode out across the plain of Sonora until they came to a region of oddly shaped bald hills among which, on the site of a natural spring, was the high-walled old monastery which had been seized from the church by Juarez's socialist government and then, when Diaz came to power, given to Don Ignacio Lazar. The monastery, with its maze of rooms, well fortified, and with its wide surrounding lands, was a valuable property. Ramón Corral had long coveted it, so when General Lazar was killed by Melody he had ordered the arrest of Lazar's two sons for an invented treason. They fled to the States and Corral seized the property for himself.

Of course, a good many of the church lands and buildings had been restored to them in order to keep the pope sweet towards the regime for the priesthood had a powerful influence over the minds of the superstitious peasantry. But some the wily Diaz hung on to to bestow as favours. Consequently half of the habitable land in Mexico now belonged to only three thousand families. It was what might be called a 'carve-up'.

The sun twinkling on the silver of their spurs, bridles, saddles, and decorated sombreros the platoon of *rurales* went prancing on their mustangs through the great wooden gates that were opened for them. When they had cared for their horses in stables that were superior by far to the abodes of most people, and filled their bellies in the vast kitchens, the *rurales* flirted with the serving wenches, or relaxed to the sound of guitar music around a fire in the great courtyard. Eventually, the fat sergeant summoned Miguel to accompany him to Ramón Corral's banqueting hall.

'I remember you!' Corral gave a roar

of laughter as he sprawled in a chair at the head of a long polished table loaded with food. 'We met in this very room a year or so ago. You and the two *gringos* agreed to fight for me. Instead you fought against us alongside those lousy Yaqui Indians.'

'That wasn't my idea,' Miguel muttered, arrogantly. 'My two *gringo* friends had an idea they were defending the oppressed. I told them there was no future in it.'

'*Si*, some *Americanos* are romantic fools.' Ramón groomed his moustaches and picked at his teeth, glancing along at his wife. 'Isn't that so, my dear?'

The pale-skinned Louisa, in a black dress threaded with gold, and diamonds about her throat, was sat quietly in the shadows. She looked up from beneath a wedge of shimmering black hair, her eyes lustrous, and met Miguel's eyes. '*Some* are.'

'Oh, yes, you two know each other.' Ramón gave a deep chuckle as he tipped back a cut-glass tumbler of ruby wine. 'I should have had you both shot, but in the mercy of my heart I have let you both live. You owe me your lives.'

'So?' Miguel shrugged and patted his revolver butt. 'What makes you think I might not use this on you?'

'You insolent dog. You stand before me and my lady without even removing your hat. I should have you flogged.'

'Does my hat bother you, Ramón?' Miguel pulled out a chair, swept off his sombrero to reveal his shiny dome, and helped himself to a glass of wine from the decanter. 'Maybe a dog obeys the man who feeds him. And I'm hungry.'

'You know how much that wine you're slopping around costs? Five hundred pesos a bottle. The best. Shipped here from France. Decanted from the barrels in my cellar. Here, have a cigar.'

Miguel chose one from the box pushed towards him, smelt it, appreciatively. 'Hmm. Better than my usual brand.'

'The best. You, you've got a damned nerve sitting there. But, I like you. You are a man who can look death in the face without flinching. I can use you.'

'I will work for anyone if the price is right. Even you, Ramón Corral.' Miguel struck a match on his boot, his spurs rattling, and gave Louisa the once over. 'Or even for your beautiful traitorous wife.'

'Traitor? What do you mean traitor? Don't push me too far. Louisa was my willing bride. We are all Mexicans. We know whose side we must be on, that of the great Don Porfirio, who has done so much for this country. We have all seen the shining light. What good are a couple of *gringo* outlaws to either of you?'

'*Si*, I agree, Your Excellency.' Miguel blew a spiral of cigar smoke in Corral's direction. 'So what do you want with me?'

'You know *el norte*? You know Texas?'

'*Si*, I have ridden both sides of

144

the border, New Mexico, Arizona, fought Comanches, Apaches, fought for lawmen and badmen.'

'I have heard of this. There is not much I do not know. You have a small, but considerable, reputation. Would you be willing to kill for me, for Mexico?'

'That depends on the price. I am looking for a nice little estate to retire to. You notice I don't ask who. If it's the President of the USA, well, I guess that could be done.'

'Miguel!' Louisa blurted out. 'You're joking.'

'No. Why should I be?'

'Don't worry, my dear. I'm not planning on killing Roosevelt.'

'Who then?'

'Get out and shut the doors,' Corral snapped at a couple of serving men, maids and two guards, and they scurried out. When they had gone he asked, 'Have you heard of the little politician?'

'Madero?'

'*Si*. He has become a thorn in our sides. He thinks he is safe in San Antonio where he stirs up the Press with his lies about Diaz. He talks nonsense about returning to our country at the head of an army.'

'If it's nonsense why worry about him?'

'Because the peasantry are gullible. He promises reforms. His name is on the mouths of everyone. They look to him as some sort of saviour. We have enough trouble already with the bandit Arango and Zapata in the south. But they are illiterates. Madero is an educated man. He has to be stopped.'

'I'm familiar with San Antonio. I've herded cattle up through Texas to the market there often enough. Nobody would pay me any heed. It's not so far over the border. Easy enough to escape from.'

'It wouldn't bother you?'

'Disposing of Madero? No he's just another dreamer spouting pie-in-the-sky panaceas like a travelling salesman.

146

I have never liked him. It would be no different to me than wringing a puppy's neck.'

'Miguel,' Louisa protested. 'Don't say that. Don't do this. Madero is a good man.'

'Haven't I warned you?' Corral sat up in his chair, a forefinger pointed at her, his face colouring up. 'How long will it take you to learn?'

'Madero is a fool,' Miguel said.

Louisa got to her feet, her dress rustling, and swept haughtily from the room. Corral scowled. 'She still has some stupid ideas in her head. I am knocking them out of her. It takes time.'

'Madero is also a very important man of international renown. There will be a big hue and cry.'

'You will be paid.' Corral reached for a carved box on the table. He took out a wad of US dollars, tossed them across, watched Miguel flick through them and give a whistle of awe. 'Five thousand. The same amount when you return, mission accomplished.'

'I would rather have land.' Miguel's dark eyes burned as he tossed his long hair at the nape of his neck over his shoulders. 'Or both.'

'You're a greedy bastard. A man after my own heart. Let me see.' He reached out for a parchment map on the table. He stabbed his finger. 'There is a nice ranch here at Alamos. Unfortunately, I had to hang the owner and his son for subversive talk. They were heard to speak support for General Huerta. He and I are not friends. Perhaps when you get back you might discreetly . . . '

'Get rid of Huerta?' Miguel shrugged. 'It would be a pleasure, Your Excellency.'

'You are unafraid of these big men?'

'They are no bigger than me. Death comes to all of us. Some sooner than others. All my life I have lived only for today. I am getting old. I need to plan for tomorrow.'

'Madero? You sure you can do this?'

Miguel pulled out his revolver, spun

the cylinder. 'Consider it done. When do I leave?'

'Tomorrow.'

'I will need ten picked men, just in case we meet up with bandits or *gringos*. It will take us a while to get to San Antonio. A month maybe. When I get there I arrange the killing. There will be no mistakes.'

'Good.' Corral roared out for the servants to return and pour them more wine. 'You and I we are the same breed. You could do well sticking by me.'

It was only after they had caroused for a while and a couple of peasant girls had been brought in to entertain them that Miguel thought of Melody. Oh, well, he sighed, she's only a whore, if not of her own choosing. Best not to press Ramón for too much too soon. He had one of the girls beneath him on the floor. 'Whores are ten a penny. Like generals in Mexico. Isn't that so, *bonita*?'

9

Mexico was a thirsty land. All too often the streams that began in the Sierra Madre trickled out into dried-up *arroyos* or salt beds. Water lay not far beneath the surface but generally the peons lacked technical know-how to irrigate their farms. Or, perhaps, the energy. The popular image in northern minds of the Mexican taking his siesta in the shade, putting pressing matters off until *mañana*, was correct, but not due to laziness. It was due to the fact that Mexico was a hungry land. Most families existed on a starvation diet of maize *tortillas* spiced with fiery peppers to make them palatable, or a plate of beans, washed down with cheap *pulque* beer. It was a land of deep, dark ignorance, which the Diaz government wished to keep that way, and from which the population only found escape through their frequent fiestas and resort to *aguardiente*, literally firewater, when a whole village, children included, would get profoundly drunk. It was also a difficult land to traverse, even the more populated and fertile San Luis Potosi being crisscrossed by mountainous chasms. Consequently, when they reached the foothills of the state of Sonora the two *gringos* found it no easy matter to get around. The land was ill-mapped. Most people knew only their nearest neighbours, so their enquiries were met by blank-faced shrugs.

Pete and Nathan did, however, manage to purchase a couple of spavined nags, and on their backs made slow progress across the land. Mainly the land was a semi-desert scrub, with which the two cowboys were familiar from their wanderings through Arizona to the north. They well knew it was wise to preserve what water they had, to shake out their boots and blankets to make sure no rattlers, scorpions, tarantulas or various nerve bugs had sought refuge, knew that they just had to keep heading on beneath the burning sun. It was a land that supported herds of scrubby cattle, but they knew that it would not do to kill one for food. They were the property of the great *haciendados*. Their *vaqueros* would have no hesitation to hang or shoot any man who tried.

'Sometimes I feel like that fella Don Quixote who rode around seeking his damsel in distress and charging at windmills,' Pete drawled as they approached another village with its slowly turning wind pump, clattered through the streets and dismounted outside a flyblown *cantina*.

'Never met the guy,' Nathan said. 'Friend of your'n?'

'Not exactly.' Pete hadn't read the book but had heard it mentioned by Southern gentlemen fellow officers when he was confined with them before Shiloh during the war. 'From what I hear Ramón Corral has taken up residence in that old monastery used to be Don Ignacio's. It ain't so far from here.'

'What we going to do? Ride up to the main gate and ask them to let us in?'

'I ain't exactly sure.' Pete settled himself at a rickety chair and table on the forecourt of the cantina which was shaded by a wattle canopy. The *patron* brought them two beers that had the taste and texture of rusty water. He could understand Nathan's sarcasm. That two broken-down *gringos* could take on Ramón Corral's horde of hired killers did seem a tad absurd. Much time had passed since that ignominious Day of the Dead in San Juan. Too much time. Days running into months and months into seasons. Time had begun to confuse him. Was it his desire to rescue his wife, Louisa, that spurred him on? Or a festering hatred and desire to kill Corral, the man who had stolen her from him? 'We'll catch up with them, somehow. Don't you worry about that, Nathan.'

'Yeah, I guess.' Nathan took a lick of salt and bite of lemon to go with the chaser of mescal, raising the cloudy liquid to his pursed lips, taking off his straw hat, and riffling fingers through his blond thatch. 'The natives ain't exactly friendly, are they?'

They could both sense the suspicion in the eyes of the dark people who peered at them from shady doorways of their cell-like *casas*, or grunted incomprehensibly at their questions.

'What would you feel if two strangers speaking a different language suddenly appeared out of nowhere?' Pete asked, as he lit a *cigarillo* and breathed out the pungent smoke. 'These are a beaten people. But don't you sense a tide waiting to turn?'

'Whaddaya mean?'

'I mean like Arango says: one day these people are going to rise up.'

'Nope,' Nathan said. 'Cain't say I see much sign of it. Uhuh!' His sentence ended in a murmured warning as he saw a group of *rurales* cantering toward the village.

'Take it easy,' Pete muttered, but he tensed and reached for the revolver on his hip to ease it in its holster. As the *rurales* noisily arrived he affected to ignore them and nonchalantly sipped at his beer.

They could not ignore for long the coarse clamour of the *rurales* who settled themselves about them at the adjoining tables, cursing and shouting, calling for refreshment, and staring at the two *Americanos* insolently. Most of these men had been common criminals, and in their new stature treated people with a swaggering contempt and cruelty.

When they saw that their ill-disguised insults and laughter was not going to ruffle the two *gringos*, one of them, a fat and greasy sergeant, placed himself before them, snapped his fingers, and demanded, 'Papers!'

Pete shrugged. 'We don't carry none.'

'You don' have? What is your business here? Who are you?'

'You know a man called Ramón Corral?'

'His Excellency? The governor? The vice president? Yes, of course I know him.'

'I mean, do you know him? Does he live around here?'

'Yes, he does. Why? What is your business?'

'We — ah — we had an appointment to meet him.' Pete took a slug of the mescal and smoke trickled from his lips. 'We got held up.'

'You?' The sergeant looked incredulously at the two bearded and scruffy *hombres* in their tight leather *chaparejos*, the worn jackets and dusty boots, the guns on their hips. 'You want to meet Señor Corral?'

'Yeah,' Nathan snarled, and pulled from his pocket the silver badge of office of Federal Bureau Investigator he ought to have given up when he resigned from the job. 'We got information for him from the United States. About Madero.'

'Madero?' The sergeant's bluster had disappeared and a worried frown appeared on his brow as he studied the badge. '*Señors*, I am a personal confidante of the governor. This is the first I have heard of this.'

'Well, it would be, wouldn't it?' Nathan said, reaching out to take back the badge. 'This is secret service stuff. He ain't likely to discuss it with the likes of you.'

'We asked you a question,' Pete said, his dark eyes boring into the Mexican. 'Where do we contact him?'

'*Señors*, I am sorry. You are too late. His Excellency has left Sonora for Mexico City. From there he goes to Santa Cruz to embark on board a ship bound for Rio de Janeiro. He will represent the president, our glorious founder, Porfirio Diaz, on a state visit to Brazil.'

'Yeah? Like when?'

'I believe they set sail today. Yes,

that's right. They'll be gone a month or more.'

'They? He's not travelling alone?'

'He is taking his young wife with him although it is hinted in the *periodicos* that she is in a delicate condition.'

'A delicate condition?' Nathan asked. 'What's he on about?'

'He means she's pregnant. Hot shee-it! That jest about caps it all.'

'*Señor*?' The sergeant's little piggy eyes were examining them. 'If you wish to wait for the vice-president's return we can escort you to Sonora and accommodate you there.'

'You can? Well, that's mighty friendly of you but our mounts ain't got the mettle of those broncs you boys are riding.'

'No problem. We have spare horses. Three of my men were killed in a brush with *bandidos* in the hills. We are returning to the city of Sonora now.'

'You are? Captain, let me buy you a drink.' Pete gave Nathan a wink as he muttered, 'This dumb bastard don't

158

seem to realize he's talking to the two most wanted *gringos* currently south of the border. Whaddya say we go along with him?'

'Suits me,' Nathan said, raising his glass to the *rurales*. 'What we got to lose? Only our lives.'

★ ★ ★

Thus it was that they rode with the *rurales* into Sonora. And thus, in the evening, after they had been lodged in the barracks, that they were led by the fat sergeant across the plaza into the back alleys of the town and into the street of the prostitutes.

'There is nothing to worry about,' the sergeant grinned, as they watched the girls in the shop windows. 'They are all medically examined and for the use of military personnel only. Tomorrow I will introduce you to the *jefe politico*, the state head of security. I am sure he would want us to take care of you.'

'I'm sure he would,' Pete agreed, scratching at his groin as a large woman, displaying her ample wares in a diaphanous gown, gave him a painted smile. '*She* looks kinda friendly, too.'

'Help yourself,' the sergeant prompted.

'Jesus Maria!' Nathan gave a low whistle. 'Do you see what I see?'

Black Pete gripped his friend's arm to warn him as he, too, saw the young woman, wearing nothing but a crisp white shirt, leaning against the back wall of the cell. Melody!

'Yeah,' he drawled. 'She's quite a peach.'

'Her?' the sergeant said, puzzled. 'She don't have enough' — he made a motion of his hands to his chest — 'woohpah! I like 'em big. That Miguel, he fancied her, too!'

'Miguel?' Nathan said, sharply. 'Who's he?'

'Some *hombre*, used to ride with the *bandidos*. He's a *rurale* now.'

'You don't say,' Nathan drawled. 'And did he have her?'

'Yeah. He said she's pretty good. You gonna try?'

'Don't mind if I do,' Nathan said, as he met Melody's startled gaze and slipped into the brightly lit room.

'Come on, *amigo*.' Pete put an arm around the sergeant and hustled him away. 'Let's go have a drink and find a real momma. Big, you know! They're welcome to these slips of gals. Man needs somethun' to get his teeth into!'

★ ★ ★

'I can't leave her there. I've got to get her out. You gonna help me?'

'How the hell we gonna do that?' Pete asked, as they sat in the barracks the next morning making the most of a breakfast of coffee, fried eggs and pancakes.

'I got an idea,' Nathan said. 'Watch out, here comes the sergeant.'

'*Buenos dias*.' The sergeant was all smiles. 'Don't forget. You meet the *jefe politico* at noon today. He should be very interested in what you have to say.'

'Yeah, I reckon he will be.' Pete was wondering what they had got themselves into. He didn't much like the tone of the sergeant's voice. There was a threat in it. Maybe they had fooled him, maybe they hadn't. But they surely wouldn't be able to fool the *jefe*, He would have accurate descriptions of them. 'Noon, you say?'

'*Si*, I will escort you to his office.'

'Hey, that gives me time to go see that li'l gal again.' Nathan got to his feet, chewing on his breakfast. 'She sure knows how to pleasure a man. You comin', boss?'

'Why not? I could do with another bite at that big lady.' He grinned and went into lurid detail of what he would do for the sergeant's benefit. 'We been out in the desert a long time. We got to make the most of this oasis.'

The sergeant gave a high-pitched giggle and joined in the coarse remarks.

'You be back before noon. I send a corporal along to escort you.'

The corporal was a short and stumpy *rurale*, who had an aggressive air befitting his rank, and carried a carbine in one hand. They strolled through the early morning marketeers to the back street where the iron gates had just been unlocked. Two soldiers on guard duty beckoned them through and smiled, for at that hour the street was more or less deserted.

When they found the shop where Melody was sitting around the stove with the other women Nathan slapped the corporal on the shoulder. The corporal had been planning to wait outside but Nathan's description of her prowess changed his mind. 'Come on in. I'll treat you. We can both have her.'

'Hang on,' Pete said. 'I think I'll join you.'

The madam seemed surprised that they all wanted Melody, but she shrugged and pocketed their pesos as they pushed the girl back into the cubicle and drew the curtain. 'These *gringos*, they're all perverts,' she said, to the amusement of the other girls. 'They like a Sonoran sandwich.'

'What's going on?' Melody hissed, as the little corporal began to unbuckle his belt.

Pete cracked him across the back of his head with the butt of his Solingen. He gave a groan and slumped on to the cot. 'Get his clothes on, quick, Melody. You're lucky, he's about your size.'

'Yeah.' Nathan peeped through the curtain. 'Hurry it up, hon. And don't forget his carbine. We're gettin' you outa here.'

Pete grinned and began to make noises as if they were enjoying themselves, Melody joined in with a few high-pitched squeals to add to the effect as she pulled off the corporal's tight velvet britches. Soon enough she was rigged out like a *rurale*, her long hair tucked up beneath his sombrero.

'You still look too damn cute.' Pete

164

stepped out of the cubicle and pushed through the whores to the stove. He picked up a coffee pot and poured himself a mugful. 'Mind if I have a drop, gal? This is damn thirsty work.'

He smilingly refused the girls' offers of assistance and, as he reached for the mug, brushed his palm across the sooty surface of the tin stove. He went back into the cubicle and wiped his hand around Melody's jaws. 'That's better. Look like you need a shave now. Let's vamoose.'

Pete tossed a handful of silver to set the whores scrabbling for it. '*Adios*, ladies.' Keeping Melody on the far side of them they noisily exited, and headed back up the hill. At the entrance gates, as they walked out, the guards casually saluted them and they headed back towards the town centre. They had hurried about a hundred yards along a narrow lane when there was a shout and, looking back, they saw the guards run out, their rifles raised. *Puh-dang!* A bullet whistled close past their heads, ricocheting off the wall.

'For Christ's sake!' Nathan shouted, pulling Melody into an alleyway. 'Run for it.' And they set off pell-mell, their boots ringing out on the cobblestones.

'Down this way,' Pete said, doubling back down another narrow lane, but they skidded to a halt when they saw one of the guards appear at the far end of it. He was taking aim with his rifle.

Without hesitation Melody faced him, her young face grim with determination not to be returned to her prison. She fired the *rurale*'s carbine from the hip and saw the guard go flying back against a wall, slowly sliding dead to the ground.

'You sure don't waste time,' Pete said, as they ran on jumping over him. 'Where the hell is the railroad station?'

'Along here,' Nathan shouted, leading the way.

When they reached a row of shops Pete paused to snatch a couple of city suits from a hanger, and two shirts, flipping a silver coin to the owner. And they went racing on, passers-by jumping like startled birds out of their path. 'We're not going to make it,' Nathan said.

'We damn well are,' Pete gritted out, looking at a clock on a bell tower. They had three seconds to go. 'A good thing we got those tickets. Still have them, Nathan?'

'Sure.' Nathan waved them as they ran into the city railroad station. There was a sharp whistle and a gasp of steam as the express began pulling out, its stack churning out smoke. A ticket collector tried to wave them down but they pushed past him and sprinted along the platform. Nathan caught up with the last carriage, opened a door, jumped inside, and held it open as the other two hurled themselves after him. They collapsed on the wooden benches, gasping for breath and grinning at each other, as clouds of smoke rolled past the open window, the train got up speed, and they went rattling on their way towards the south.

'Whee-hooo!' Nathan hugged an arm around the neck of his 'rurale', pulling her into him. 'That was one narrow squeak. There ain't another train for three days.'

Pete looked out of the window. There didn't appear to be any sign of pursuit. 'Luck seems to be with us. But you never can tell. When you two have quit hugging each other we had better split up, keep our heads down, get out of these *bandido* duds. Right this moment you look like a couple of them molly boys kissin' each other.'

'I don't care,' Melody cried. 'I'm so happy.'

10

'How long we gonna hang around here waiting for Arango to show up?' Nathan asked, as they sat in a bar in Durango City.

'This is where he told me to wait. I've given a message to the barkeep.'

'How do you know you can trust him?'

'I don't,' Pete growled. 'There are spies everywhere. But there's also an underground grapevine. We'll give him a while longer.'

He had had his ragged mane of black hair shorn short, was clean shaven, and in his city suit looked like any other city-dweller, if he hadn't towered head and shoulders over most Mexicans. He stared gloomily at a half-empty bottle of mescal before him. It was an evil drink, made him edgy and paranoid. He had begun to think that everywhere people were watching him.

He knew he needed to pull himself off it before it began to get a hold of him. But he filled himself another glass full. The news about Louisa had disheartened him.

Nathan, too, had adopted a clean-cut image in his city clothes, and had his hair darkened. Only their boots and spurs marked them out as horsemen, but that was not unusual. Melody had thrown away her *rurale* outfit, and reverted to blouse, skirt, poncho and sombrero. In contrast to Pete they looked radiantly happy to be back together. But they were also restless to get away from this down-trodden country where Diaz had created the first modern totalitarian police state. They possessed new forged papers and so far had avoided suspicion, but they could never be truly at ease.

'You two don't have to hang around for me. Why don't you head back to the States?'

Nathan glanced at Melody. 'Why don't you come with us?'

'Maybe I will. There ain't much point in looking for Louisa at present. I sure ain't gonna go down to Brazil.'

'I ain't so sure you're ever going to get her back, Pete. Why don't you forget Corral, forget Arango?'

'Talk of the devil,' Pete muttered, for crossing the plaza was a stocky, pigeon-toed man with curly hair and heavy jowls. He was wearing a dusty, ill-fitting suit, tight across his broad shoulders and belly, but there was no mistaking him. 'Look who it ain't.'

Arango pushed through the beaded curtain of the door, carefully studied all present through narrowed eyes, slapped Pete's shoulder and sat beside him. 'Good to see you, *amigos*. You see to that business you had to?'

'Part of it,' Pete said, nodding at Melody. 'My part's still missing. How are things with you, Doroteo?'

'Hsst! That isn't a name I recognize any more. Arango is dead. He had become too well known. I have taken a new name, Villa. You can call me Pancho.'

'Pancho Villa,' Pete mused, offering his hand. 'Pleased to meetcha. It's got a good ring to it. Maybe one day the world will hear more of it.'

'Maybe they will. Support for the cause is growing everywhere. I want you to go get Madero. I fear for his life in Texas. He would be safer here with me in Mexico. At the head of my army. The time is ready. We cannot wait. You must persuade him of that.'

★ ★ ★

San Antonio. It was not exactly the safest place for Pete Bowen. There was a price on his head in Texas. He was wanted by the Rangers and the Pinkerton Detective Agency. When his wife had been murdered by the Murchisons, his ranch-house burned down, and, himself half-hanged,[1] he

---

[1] *See* Death at Sombrero Rock

172

had put his young son on the stage to go live with an aunt in Kansas, walked into the San Antonio Cattlemen's Club and shot Old Man Murchison dead. To kill the richest cow baron in Texas was not an act that was easily forgotten.

He set off north on the railroad with Nathan and Melody, crossing the border by way of Laredo. His new city look and forged papers did the trick, and he went unchallenged by any border guard or lawman. Nathan breathed a sigh of relief to be back in the land of the free because he was now no longer on anybody's wanted list.

'You two are free to go wherever you want. You can get your share of the silver we sold out of the Wells Fargo bank. I don't want you to feel you're beholden to me.'

'You're not going back, are you?' Nathan asked. 'Why bother about Madero?'

'I gave my word to Arango — I mean what's he call himself, Pancho Villa — and I'm going to need his help if I'm ever going to get Louisa out alive.'

'Aw, shoot, Nathan. We gotta stay with Pete. We're all in this together.'

'I'm telling you I don't want you with me. Go now. Make a life for yourselves. Settle down. Have some damn kids.'

'We're staying with you,' Nathan said. 'We've always stuck together. We'll see this through. I guess we'll split the cash three ways now Miguel's gone on the other side.'

'Yeah, I guess,' Pete said, wearily. 'I never thought . . . he always was a hard fella to fathom.'

'Maybe he's biding his time with the *rurales*, playing them along.'

'No, I don't think so,' Melody said. 'He is a hard man. He told me that nothing stays the same. He's a hired gun at heart.'

'Yeah, waal, you couldn't help liking him all the same,' Pete said. 'He was a helluva character.'

They had this conversation as the

train took them north across the parched Texan plain to San Antonio. They didn't have any trouble finding Madero. In spite of the coming of the railroad it was still much the same dusty old town, its central plaza packed with wagons and market stalls as people brought their produce in from far and wide, and bellowing longhorns waited forlornly in the cattle pens for transportation to the northern markets. 'It sure beats trailing them a thousand miles up across the Red River and through Injun Territory to Kansas,' Pete said. 'Times sure are changing.'

Madero and his aides were shacked up on the top floor of Jordan's Hotel. The only trouble was persuading him to return with them to Mexico. His fiery articles in the journals preaching revolution were one thing, when it came to putting them into practice he took on the look of a frightened mouse in his shiny suit and pince nez spectacles.

'He just won't make up his mind,'

Pete reported. 'I'm half-inclined to slug him over the head and take him back by force. I sure don't like hanging about in this town. Too many folk know me.'

★ ★ ★

Miguel and his men had set out before Pete and crossed the border into Texas near Piedro Negras. They travelled by horseback and made good progress until they passed through Fort Inge on the Rio Frio. There they were surrounded by a posse of townspeople and Rangers. Outnumbered and outgunned, they surrendered. They were accused of being rustlers and thrown in the lock-up. They kicked their heels for two weeks, protesting their innocence, vehemently claiming they had come north to buy horses. At their trial, as there was no solid evidence against them, the judge, reluctantly, ordered their release. They rode on feeling lucky they hadn't been lynched, Miguel chafing at the waste of time.

In San Antonio he was informed Madero was staying at Jordan's Hotel. They said he was in the habit of venturing out for a constitutional first thing in the morning with a couple of his aides. Miguel took a room in a hotel nearby.

* * *

Madero had finally stopped dithering and decided to return to Chihuahua with Pete to meet Pancho Villa. He had packed his bags, his typewriter and his pamphlets, and booked tickets on the train out the next morning. Pete, Nathan and Melody went along to the hotel to meet him.

'Hell fire!' Miguel hissed out, when he looked from the window of his second-storey room and saw them. 'What are they doing here?'

For moments he was half-inclined to call the mission off and go join them. His muddy eyes flickered his concern as he watched them enter Jordan's Hotel. But he had taken Corral's $5,000 and shaken on the deal. He was a man of his word and one of considerable determination. He had posted six of his men at windows and on the rooftops of the row of flat-roofed adobe houses that faced the hotel. Their combined fire should not fail to cut Madero down. Nor was he sure he had time to call his wild dogs off even if he had wanted to. The others were down in the street waiting with fresh horses ready to ride the 150 miles back to the Mexican border.

Miguel licked his lips with indecision. He had known Pete, Nathan and Melody a long time, but this was business. A small fortune was at stake. Pete Bowen was a good man, but he had never got anywhere riding with him. Miguel was not unwary of his former friends' ability with guns. He, however, had double their number and the advantage of surprise. He determined there could be no going back. He would have to shoot to kill. Carefully he adjusted the front and rear sights of the high-powered bolt-action Browning he had brought along for this job. It was specially chambered to take a large .284 cartridge with what they called a dum-dum head. It would tear apart a man's body, twisting inside him. There was talk of making it illegal it made such a mess. He took a bead on the front steps of the main door of the hotel and waited . . .

Pete came out of the hotel at the head of the Madero party. There appeared to be just the usual coming and going along the wide dusty street of wagons, buggies and horsemen, a peaceful early morning scene. A small group of Mexicans were sitting with their horses further along. Not an unusual sight in southern Texas. Probably *vaqueros*. He wondered why they were hanging on to some spare saddled horses. Maybe waiting for their comrades to come from a saloon. Expensive saddles. He could see the glint of the sun on the silver of pommels. Most ordinary *vaqueros* couldn't afford fine saddles like that. Maybe it was this made him look apprehensively at the row of houses opposite. And he saw the sun glinting on the gold-plated trigger of a rifle at a bedroom window.

'Get down!' he shouted to the little Madero, who was following him down the steps of the hotel. Pete grabbed hold of his suit lapel, saw his startled expression as he dragged him down beneath the hooves of a horse at the hitching rail. Simultaneously, bullets splintered the wood of the steps where seconds before he had been standing, smashing holes in it. One of his aides gave a piercing scream as he was hit, blood gouting from the hole torn by the dum-dum in his chest. All hell broke loose.

Pete crawled along behind the whinnying, kicking horse, dragging Madero with him, aiming for the shelter of a water trough. He pulled his Solingen revolver, firing up at a shadowy figure in the bedroom window. There was a flash of gunfire as whoever it was continued to pump out bullets from a high-powered rifle. Another of Madero's companions groaned his last as his life was splattered out of him. Melody died instantly as a dum-dum slug took her apart.

Nathan shouted out his frustration and grief as, soaked with blood, others of the party panicked to get back into the hotel. He could see men firing from the rooftops of the 'dobes, but they had the sun behind their backs and provided hazy targets. He kneeled beside Melody and emptied his Colt at them in rage, relieved to see two tumble into the dust.

The men on their fiery mustangs galloped down the street to join in the attack as people ran out of the way. Nathan snatched up Melody's fallen carbine and pumped out bullets at them, joyously watching as they were blasted from their saddles, and horses were brought crashing down.

181

Somebody above him, at an upstairs window of Jordan's Hotel, was helping out, firing a rifle at the men on the flat-roofed adobes. One tried to seek better cover, was hit, pirouetted on the edge and keeled over, bouncing on a canopy to hit the dust with a thud, lying lifeless.

'Stay here,' Pete shouted, thrusting Madero's face into the dirt. He reloaded his revolver, forcing himself to concentrate amid the noise and confusion, the rolling clouds of gunpowder and explosions. Then he was up and racing across the road to the adobes. He kicked in a door and went in, his revolver in readiness.

In the room above Miguel cursed as he slammed back the bolt of his Browning to feed another slug into the breech. Things were not going well. He wanted to get in a shot at Madero and reckoned he was cowering behind the water trough. If he was, his powerful slugs could easily plough through it. But Nathan, kneeling on the hotel steps with his carbine, was making things too hot for him. He narrowed his eyes and scowled as chips of baked adobe showered him and bullets whined through the window. It was kill or be killed. Nathan had to be stopped. Miguel took careful aim and saw his slug bowl the blond Texan cowboy over. He lay on top of Melody, his blood seeping out of him.

'Miguel!'

Miguel spun round, saw the tall figure of Pete Bowen standing in the doorway behind him, saw his Solingen spurt flame as he, himself, squeezed the gold-plated trigger of his Browning. The slug hit Miguel full in the chest and he was hurled back out of the window. Pete relaxed, went to look down, and saw him sprawled amid the carnage in the street.

His revolver smoking in his hand Pete walked back across to the hotel. He looked down at Nathan and Melody, the dark pools of blood oozing from them on to the wooden porch to drip through to the dust below, the rictus of death's agony on their faces. He knelt to close their eyes and blinked away tears in his own as he muttered, 'What a waste.'

Madero was visibly shaking as a crowd of rubber-neckers gathered round and he examined his dead comrades. Only one had escaped back into the hotel. 'The sheriff's outa town,' somebody said.

Pete glowered at them. 'You can all see what happened. These hired assassins tried to kill Mr Madero here. And managed to kill my friends in the process.' He peeled a hundred dollar bill from a roll and handed it to a black-clothed undertaker who had already started measuring up the bodies. 'Their names were Nathan Stone and his wife, Melody. I want you to give 'em a good burial. And headstone.'

He turned to Madero. 'Grab hold your bag. We can still catch that train. I figure you'll be safer in Mexico.'

The mayor of San Antonio came

bustling up. 'You all have to make statements concerning this. You all have to wait for the return of the sheriff.'

'We ain't got time,' Pete said, and pressed the mayor aside with a forefinger.

The crowd parted. Nobody seemed to want to argue with the tall, dark-eyed stranger with the revolver on his hip.

Pete rolled over Miguel with his boot-tip and studied the dark head, as if hewn from mahogany, the lifeless eyes.

'You ride and fight alongside a man for years and you never know him,' he whispered. 'Never know what a man will do for cash. Kill his own buddies.'

He picked up the Browning rifle, studied it and tucked it under his arm. '*Adios, amigo,*' he said sadly.

There was the howl of a locomotive's steam whistle approaching over the plain from the direction of Houston.

185

'Come on,' he said, and ambled off down the street towards the depot, Madero and his friend hurrying along behind him.

'That fellow,' a man said, standing on the sidewalk and watching him go. 'I'm sure I seen him before.'

'That's Black Pete Bowen,' another replied. 'There's been a price on his head for years.'

11

A seething crowd of Villa-istas greeted the train as it rolled into Chihuahua, men, bristling with arms, on wild mustangs, firing revolvers into the air, cotton-clad peons holding ancient rifles, running forward to clamber onto the carriages, clamouring to see Francisco Madero. The little 'chocolate fool' looked startled. When he heard the gunfire he had thought they must be bandits. He had not expected such a reception.

'This rabble's your army,' Pete said, taking his arm and leading him to the door of the compartment. 'You'd better start acting like their saviour.'

Madero straightened his celluloid collar and suit, and saluted them. He was hauled from the steps of the locomotive and hoisted shoulder high. They carried him through the shouting throng towards Pancho Villa and his henchmen, who sat on horse-back. A free horse was brought forward and Madero, not an expert rider, was placed on top of it. He perched there, anxiously, as Villa roared, 'President Madero! With him we will ride to victory!'

There was a great celebration that night as even the poorest of peons vied to go forward and present some small gift they could ill afford, to kneel for the privilege of touching Madero's hand.

Pete was invited to feast alongside Villa, but as he lit a cheroot, took a swig of mescal, and stretched his long legs, he looked a trifle dubious as he listened to Madero.

'My children,' Madero shrilled at the hushed crowd. 'This is the beginning. We are but a stream. Soon we will be a river. Mexico can no longer suffer under the lash of a dictator. Here in Chihuahua Don Luiz Terrazas holds sway, the richest and most hated landowner in the state. Why should he own seventy million acres when you have nothing? I hear that he has raised a private army in the south for Diaz to attack us. We will fight back. We will defeat him. With Pancho Villa by my side there is no doubt of that. When I become president all his land will be divided among you. I give you my word.'

Each sentence was greeted by ecstatic cheers so it was difficult to hear the next one. The benign little politician sat back as the raucous trumpets of a town band burst forth, and girls, with castanets and tambourines, were brought forward to dance for him. Pete had heard enough of the eulogies. He eased himself out of the throng, and wandered through the streets where everywhere parties were in progress. When he was recognized he was greeted as a conquering hero. A bottle stuck in his belt, and a willing *señorita* on each arm even the melancholy Texan was fired by talk of revolution. It was quite a night.

★ ★ ★

But the war was far from won. A year of horror had begun, burning, looting, hangings, torture, as Don Luis's brigade, ably assisted by the hardened *rurales* and soldiers tried to pin down Villa's troops, attacking them on all sides.

If Parra had been known as The Puma, Villa became the Black Jaguar of the North, a tribute to his cunning in outwitting the *federales* in the mountains of northern Chihuahua.

An odd nickname, perhaps, for the black jaguar was virtually extinct in Northern America. Hemmed in on all sides, Pete had little option but to ride alongside Villa, to help blow bridges and rails, to attack silver trains, and armoured wagons, to steal weapons, to rustle cattle from across the border and to execute all who opposed them. The military was not their only adversary. In the coming summer they had to contend with the worst drought in recent history as the peasants' meagre crops failed and their wells dried up. The customary famine increased fourfold. The sight of a woman dead from starvation with a child at her milkless breast became commonplace. If Villa was grossly cruel to his enemies, he was generous to those who supported him. He began to concentrate his actions on capturing cattle, grain and provisions to distribute among the peons who hid them, spied for them, and misdirected pursuers. And everywhere they rode small towns welcomed his arrival with shouts of 'Villa! Villa!' The former bandit chieftain, unschooled and illiterate, was unwittingly abandoning brigandage to be the idealistic leader of social revolution.

Everywhere the message of Madero and Villa was being taken up and, if the country had not splintered into warring factions led by almost anyone who could command a few guns and horsemen, victory would have come sooner. In Chihuahua Pancho Villa joined forces with Pasqual Orozco, a bandit chief and revolutionary, and together they attacked the military. From all parts of the territory men, women, and mere boys arrived to support them, carrying stolen pistols, or simply machetes, on foot, on burros, clinging to the roofs and sides of trains, they rose up like a tidal wave to follow Madero, common soldiers deserting, tearing off their uniforms to join this barefoot, ragged army. By sheer weight of numbers, and the fervour of their feeling, they chased Don Luis, the *rurales* and *federales* out of the state.

By the end of the summer the jauntily cheerful Villa was virtual ruler of Chihuahua. He togged himself out in a general's uniform and cap, gave Orozco a generalship and 50,000 pesos, and made plans with Madero to unite with revolutionary forces to the south, in Durango and San Luis Potosi, and to sweep on to Mexico City.

Pete declined a generalship, himself.

He had witnessed much fanatical bravery by the common people, and had been inspired to ride alongside Villa in the vanguard. But he was sickened by the wanton killing, the madness of it all, even the crazed celebrations as they took yet another town. Madero, too, appeared to be lost and puzzled amid it all. Putting into practice his Utopian ideals in such a place as Mexico was going to be very difficult, if not impossible. All about him men were offering advice, demanding rewards. He would have to put off land reforms until he had achieved an alliance with Emiliano Zapata in the tropical south, and the scheming General Huerta and his forces to the east. As for Pete, he decided it was time to leave them to their bickering and go take a look for Louisa.

12

Ramón Corral, in pearl-encrusted velveteens and wide sombrero, was watching the black bulls being tried in the adobe arena he had had built outside the monastery. 'Look at that beauty!' A lithe creature, muscles rippling beneath its glossy hide, pawed the sand, snorted his anger and charged like an arrow from a bow. The banderilla barely managed to escape the vicious horns, but leapt deftly aside, played the bull with a cape and raced for safety. The bull hammered at the wooden escape door and, head held high, went trotting defiantly around the ring seeking other tormentors.

'We will keep him for the final fight,' Ramón told his manager, cracking his bullwhip across the haunches of the beast as he passed and laughing at his anger. 'Tomorrow he will die.'

Six bulls had been chosen. A famous matador and his troupe would be visiting to entertain the crowd. Various bigwigs and rich ranchers had been invited, and peons would flock from far and wide to see the show. The celebration was in honour of his and Louisa's baby son.

About a mile away, on the crest of one of the bald hills, Pete Bowen lay in the rocks and watched through an eyeglass. He picked up Miguel's bolt-action Browning rifle and squinted along the sights. With a little luck he could blast Corral off the wall and into his own bullring. He fingered the gold-plated trigger and sighed. For the second time in his life he let him live. It would not serve his purpose.

Pete picked up the brass telescope again as he saw an ornately gilded coach, drawn by six horses, leave the gates of the monastery and proceed around the walls through the peons' boxy *casas* until it reached the bullring.

A young woman, her white dress billowed by the breeze, stepped out. She had a baby in her arms. Pete bit his lip. Louisa!

He frowned as he watched Ramón jump down to greet her, putting out an arm to draw her to him, and dibbling a finger to play with the swaddled infant. Pete put the glass aside and rubbed his eye as the image became misty. 'Hell, I'm gettin' old,' he muttered. 'My eyesight ain't what it used to be.'

He kept watch on them for a good while as they dallied and the fierce bulls were herded by *vaqueros* on mustangs back to their corral. He saw Corral and Louisa climb back into the coach. Maybe this was his chance to strike . . . if they were going on a journey. But the coach made a cumbersome turn, went through the monastery's portals, and the great gates were closed. How the hell am I gonna get in that fortress? he wondered. He could see sentries perched at intervals on the top of the walls.

Pancho Villa's rabble-rousing revolution had not yet reached this side of the Sierra Madre, although there was a strong undercurrent of feeling against Ramón Corral in the state of Sonora. Corral was taking no chances. His home was as closely guarded as Fort Knox.

The sun lowered, the night grew chill, and Pete returned on his bronc to the hut of the shepherd who had given him shelter the previous night. He had told him he was a *Yanqui* prospecting for silver. The shepherd welcomed him, watered and gave corn to his horse, for Pete's pesos were much needed. The hut was just a tumbledown shack where he lived and slept in one room with his wife and children. There was no door but a skin, no chairs, no table, nothing of any value but a few clay pots and wooden utensils. In other words, it was much the same as any other peon's hovel throughout Mexico. The woman kneaded maize into a dough and flapped it between her palms until it became a thin tortilla to be fried and eaten with yams and beans. To have roasted one of their scrubby flock would have been regarded as a great luxury. But impossible. The family lived in a state of feudal dependency on the vast estate of Corral. They had to account to his overseer for every sheep they grazed.

'You going to the bullfight tomorrow?' Pete asked, as he squatted on a coarse mat around the open hearth of the stone oven. He smiled at the children, the woman, and the shepherd, who were huddled in their ponchos for warmth, amid dogs, and a couple of sheep with lambs who had been brought in for safety from prowling predators.

'*Si*, of course.' The shepherd poured Pete a mug of cactus *pulque* and accepted one of his cigarettes. 'We must drink the health of His Excellency, his new wife and child. He provides the best bullfights in Sonora. They say they are better than in Mexico City.'

'Bread and games. He buys your allegiance like the Roman emperors used to do.'

'Why not?' The shepherd sucked in smoke and shrugged. 'What else is there?'

'You don't mind that you and your children are more or less slaves?'

'What can we do?' The shepherd stared at the embers of the small fire, fatalistically.

'Haven't you heard of Madero and Pancho Villa?'

'*Si*, we have heard. But in Sonora the *rurales* are everywhere. Villa will never get anywhere.'

'You think so?' Again Pete smiled through his thin lips, ruefully. 'Waal, I guess I'll go take a look at the bullfight, myself. There's nothing like a little fiesta.'

He laid the Solingen double-action between his thighs as he slept, and the Browning close at hand, but the night brought no disturbance apart from the foetid smells, the noises of the animals and humans crammed together in that tiny cell.

* * *

In the morning sunshine he asked the shepherd if he could buy some cotton clothes. The shepherd produced shirt and baggy pants, with a sash, that had belonged to his father. They were a bit of a tight fit, and the pants only reached to his mid-calves, which, fortunately, were still bronzed from the time he crossed the mountains. He was tall, but in rope-soled *huraches* and a straw sombrero he might pass as a Mexican.

'It's a more comfortable get-up in the heat,' Pete explained. 'And we *gringos* ain't popular due to all the land concessions and special privileges your president has given us. I like to keep a low profile.'

The shepherd shrugged once more and accepted the pesos. It was well-known all *gringos* were crazy.

200

'I'll leave my horse and rifle here. They'll be safe?'

'*Señor, mi casa es su casa*. You are our guest.'

'Good,' Pete grunted.

It seemed to him his best approach in getting Louisa out would be to use stealth. He had little hope of fighting his way through Corral's formidable bodyguard.

★ ★ ★

He felt uneasy as he strolled with the family towards the monastery. Uneasy and foolish. He had tied the Solingen into his poncho, which he had draped over his shoulder. But what good would a handful of bullets be against 200 *rurales*? He had begun to rue the day he had ever come to Mexico. The death of his friends, Nathan and Melody, weighed heavily on him. And even the death of their murderer, Miguel. It seemed that death followed him everywhere.

He had lost count long ago of the men he had killed. From an early age he had learned how to defend himself. In the victory and then despair at Shiloh he had seen his comrades cut down, so many it did not seem possible, the grass stained red with their blood. As a Confederate lieutenant he had led a doomed brigade of Cherokee Light Cavalry, made brave and bitter guerrilla rear-guard actions as the Federals flooded into Indian Territory until his men were hounded down and shot like animals. At the age of twenty he had crossed the Great American Desert, Utah and Nevada, seeking gold in Virginia City, and got entangled with a crooked, beautiful card-sharp and seen her die. He had fought Comanches who attacked his ranch in Texas, the Comancheros who supplied them with rifles, and Murchison's boys who tried to run him off his land. He had seen his wife burn. It was like everyone he loved, even his horses, ended up dead. He had herded cattle to the roistering railroad towns of Kansas, and made a name for himself among the fast guns of Abilene, Dodge and Newton, outshooting more men than he cared to remember. He had trailed mad dog badmen through No Man's Land, tangled with Billy the Kid and his boys in New Mexico, and, as an outlaw, himself, been forced to hand out arbitrary justice to any who opposed him, or tried to track him down. He had ridden south into Mexico in the hope of finding some respite from fighting. Some hope! Trouble followed him wherever he went.

As they walked towards the *haciendado*'s monastery they were joined by trickles of other peons heading towards there for the bullfight until they became a wide stream of people, some on foot, some on burros. In spite of their jollity and greetings to one another, Pete's thoughts remained morose, somewhat self-pitying and death-fixated as he mingled with them and tried, under his sombrero, to appear inconspicuous amid the throng. As they drew near the ancient monastery reared over them. Just how, he wondered, was he going to get in?

Occasionally, the river of peons parted to allow elegantly adorned guests in open landaus, in light buggies, or on spirited horses, among their retainers, to go trotting through them. Pretty girls, flowers in their dark hair, in gay, ruffled dresses, went along clinging to their beaux who were in stiff-brimmed hats and traditional, flashy outfits of Spanish cavaliers. They laughed and smiled, so far above the ordinary peasants they might have been visitors from another world.

These fortunate few were welcomed to the seats in the shade of the arena around the vice-president's box. Pete paid a few pesos for the privilege of sitting among the hoi polloi in the heat of the afternoon sun. Just before four o'clock there was a ripple of excitement as Corral and his lady arrived to take their seats. Some, who were aware of his murderous reputation, smiled frigidly. Others broke into rapturous applause.

Pete sat on the hard stone and studied Louisa. She was dressed exquisitely in the height of city fashion, a high-necked dress of white lace over satin, her dark hair swept up beneath a wide be-flowered hat, her hands in long lace gloves. He saw her poise, the gracefulness of her long, slender neck, the shadowed cut of her pale cheek, the fullness of her bosom beneath the dress, the woman he loved, who should be his. There was a great fanfare of trumpets from the orchestra, and cries and shouts as the matadors and their attendants marched into the sandy arena, in their 'suits of lights', tightly swathed like dolls, but walking with the arrogance of men who knew they were above ordinary mortals, their heads held high, a sway to their hips, men who had come to defy death. When they reached Corral's be-flagged box the leading matador bowed and tossed a bouquet of flowers to Louisa. It cut into Pete's heart, for some reason, as he saw her easily catch it and flash a smile in response.

There was a great roar from the crowd as the first bull spurted into the ring. More bloodthirsty roars as the broad-shouldered picador held back the bull's thrashing weight with his lance, as the horse screamed its fear. And great huzzahs of '*Olé*' as the matador swirled his cape, the bull and man became one, and he guided it in a dance of death. Until at last it stood blood-let and bewildered before him, a conquered beast, and he faced up to it, and thrust home the sword.

No need to record six such kills. It wasn't exactly Pete's cup of coffee. He began to feel kinda squeamish as the show went on. But Louisa appeared to be elated, the centre of attention. The matador tossed her more flowers, and handed her the blood-dripping ears. Could this be the Louisa he knew?

She appeared strangely at ease in the role of the ruling lady.

The ancient ritual of the bulls over, the peons gathered at the back of the ring to watch their no longer noble carcasses hoisted on hooks and carved up. If they were lucky they might be thrown scraps of offal.

Others had begun dancing and drinking, but with a dark, desperate seriousness on their carved Mayan faces, as if seeking the bliss of oblivion. Groups of men with guitars, pan pipes and drums, roughly hand-made, began to play stirring rhythms, as the people about them stamped and clapped their hands.

Ramón Corral, Louisa, and a retinue of friends, with a cohort of *rurales* all about, strolled through the throng, Corral calling out and slapping the shoulders of a few he knew by name, Louisa smiling radiantly at peasant women with babies strung at their backs, or ruffling the hair of little guttersnipes. Four barrels of wine were unloaded from a wagon hauled by oxen, and Corral made a great show of knocking out the bungs, and drinking a toast to the president, their great benefactor. It was far from his best stuff and he could afford to be generous. Wasn't he celebrating the birth of his first, at least that is to say, legitimate son?

The said infant, swathed in lacy wrappings, was brought out from a coach by his nanny, and Louisa held him in her arms, as Ramón splashed wine about and toasted his son and heir. Pete kept in the background, but at one point Louisa passed so close he could have reached out and touched her.

By this time it was dusk, and Ramón and Louisa climbed into their big golden coach and six, and led a procession of their principal guests back into the monastery where a great banquet was to be served. They did not know that Pete was hanging to the struts below a few inches from the dusty ground, and watching the hooves of the horses. As the coach came to a halt in the inner courtyard he rolled out from beneath and slipped away into the darkness

★ ★ ★

The banquet was a long-winded affair of many courses and speeches. Louisa noticed that Ramón was getting drunk and garrulous, his words sometimes greeted with silence, especially by the small group of foreigners who had been invited to the event. He was not a very popular man. He had had bad publicity. And now he was making a fool of himself.

In responding to a toast to President Diaz, an American mine-owner remarked, 'In view of the events taking place in Chihuahua and elsewhere, the social unrest in your country, we of the international community would be glad of some assurances. We have invested a lot of finance into Mexico and, while admittedly, President Diaz has been more than generous in his allotment of land, and the special terms offered us, we are naturally concerned for the safety of ourselves and our companies. Can we be given an assurance — '

'What assurance do you need?' Corral lurched to his feet, his voice heavy with wine. 'You talk about Pancho Villa? He is nothing. A braggart. A *bandido*. Madero? A jumped-up little worm. We will deal with them in our own time. Our own way. You *gringos*, you don' understand — '

He slipped and had to support himself on the table as a barrage of questions were shot at him by the Americans. He frowned as Louisa rose, fanning herself. 'My wife wishes to excuse herself. You know she has not been too well.' The men got to their feet, respectfully as she walked out, and then began shouting again.

★ ★ ★

To avoid the maze of passages, no doubt peopled at intervals by *rurale* guards, Pete had worked his way around the outside of the monastery building until he reached the rocky jut at its far end, like the prow of a ship. In the darkness he dug his fingers and toes into its almost sheer face and worked his way up. The climb was made easier by the lightness of his clothes and his rope soles. He reached the balcony and, peering over to make sure the coast was clear, swung over. Sure enough, there was the great swimming bath carved into the rock, that great luxury in so thirsty a land, dug for the *haciendado* to take his morning bathe. He remembered it as the pool where Melody had drowned the evil old lecher, Don Ignacio. The water glistened in the moonlight, empty now.

There was a dim light from within the master bedroom and *haciendado*'s suite of rooms that opened on to the balcony. Pete had only a hazy plan in his head. He would find Louisa, kill Ramón Corral and anyone who tried to step in their way, and take her away from this cursed land, take her to the USA. As for the child, he was not sure whether it might not be best to leave him here. It would not be easy getting away. He had found a long coil of rope in the courtyard and had carried it slung over his shoulder. He planned to use it to make their descent down the steep monastery wall. Once away, he would steal spare horses, and escape with her north across the Sonoran plain. The frontier was not so far away.

He tossed the rope into a corner and edged over to a door. It was securely locked. But a window was a different kettle of fish. He smashed it with an elbow, put his hand through, unleased the catch. He listened. There was no sound so he stepped through.

It was some kind of dressing-room, full of bottles of unguents and powders, and expensive gewgaws and clothes scattered in profusion about the chairs and divans. Pete froze as the door swung open and Louisa's personal maid appeared. He pulled her inside and put his hand over her mouth. Her eyes bulged up at him as he signalled her to be silent, emphasizing the request with the barrel of his revolver moved across her lips. She gave only a gasp of fear as he released her. He signalled her to sit on a chair and bound her hand and foot with sashes. He tied a tight gag on her as he heard a female voice call out, 'Maria? What are you doing in there?'

He went to the door and saw that she was half-sitting on the four-poster bed in a satin night-dress. She was brushing out her long black hair and it shimmered in the candlelight.

'Louisa,' he called, and his voice was husky with longing.

She spun round, one elbow crooked, holding her hair back, and her eyes blazed like a cornered puma. Her face drained of colour, as pale as ice, as she hissed, 'Pete?'

He gave an awkward scoffing smile.

'Kinda surprised?'

She did not reply, but sat and clutched at the bedcover, staring at him. He strode to a couple of adjoining doors and peered through them. He seemed satisfied there was no one within earshot. He stuffed the revolver back in his belt. 'Come to get you out,' he said.

'Get me out?' she repeated, her eyes fixed on him from their wide whites. 'What do you mean?'

'Take you away from here. You couldn't have doubted I'd try, surely?'

'No. You're crazy enough to try. I always knew that. Ramón would never let us get away. He would hunt us down.'

'Come on,' Pete said. 'Get your clothes on. We gotta get started. I got a rope. We can get down the walls in cover of darkness.'

He pulled her up and held her to him, the shimmering softness of her nightdress, the warmth of her body, the lustre of her eyes, her hair, bringing back deep memories. He wanted to take her then and there. But there would be time enough for that.

Louisa steeled herself against him, pressing her palms against his chest. 'Pete, it's no good. You go. Get out while you can.'

He grasped her hard to him, sought her lips. 'Louisa, it's me. We can do this.'

She turned her face away. 'What are you doing?' She seemed to gag on the words, as if she could hardly get them out. 'It's different. I'm different. I'm a married woman. Married in front of a huge congregation. Married in the eyes of God. Do you think I would leave my child?'

'Where is he? We'll take him with us.'

'Don't be absurd. How could we? There are *rurales* out in that corridor. You would never get past them.'

'You go and get him. I'll tuck him into my shirt and we'll climb down. We can do this, Louisa. Go on.'

She sat back on the bed and stubbornly shook her head. 'I love you, Pete. I did love you. But you are a fool. It would never work. Do you think I'm going to risk my child's life?'

'Louisa,' he insisted. 'Look at me. Nathan and Melody are dead. But we have a chance to make a new life. Come with me.'

When she still dumbly shook her head he asked, 'Whose child is he? Mine or Ramón's?'

'Ramón's. He was born a year after you — after they sent you away. I'm glad you're alive, Pete. Go away. Now. Quickly. Forget me.'

'I kinda figured he was.' Her words, her resistance, was like a knife in the chest. 'But, still, I can be his father. Surely you don't want to stay with Corral. He is a cold-blooded murderer. He is an evil man.'

'You have killed men, too,' she said. 'In war, I realize now, things have to be done. He forced me. I didn't want to, believe me. I fought. How I fought!

But all that is over. We are married. He is my husband. Underneath he is not such a bad man.'

'What about our marriage? By Father Francisco? Doesn't that count?'

'Father Francisco had no right to marry us. He was excommunicated. We were never legally wed.'

'Aw, Jesus! You goin' to throw away all we had? This is our chance, Louisa. Take it. Go on. Get the kid.'

She smiled, and gave a little gasp, as an outer door banged. 'It's too late,' she said.

'Louisa!' Ramón called, as he burst through the door. And he stood, his shoulders hunched, and stared like a flummoxed bull. 'What in hell's going on?'

'Howdy, Ramón,' Pete said, the Solingen .44 aimed at his heart. He stood, one arm pressing Louisa back. 'I've come to collect my wife.'

'Your wife? She is the wife of the Vice-President of Mexico. Soon maybe the wife of the president of Mexico.

She is not the wife of some scum of the sewers, some saddle-tramp outlaw, some *bandido*.'

'Yeah, spit it out. They're gonna be the last words you do say, you bag of shit. It's gonna be a pleasure to see the blood pump out of you. Ain't you aware you're the most hated man in Mexico? Are you blind to what a pig you are? Why should she want to stay with you?'

'For all this.' Ramón cast his arms around the ostentatiously furnished bedroom. 'For my riches, my lands, my position. Louisa is somebody in life. You think she wants to go back to live in a hovel? With some *gringo* trash?'

'Ramón!' Louisa called out, sharply. 'Don't.'

'Don't what?' he growled, and spread his hands open, dropping them towards the guns on his hips, as if he was suicidally planning to draw against the Texan, one of the fastest gunfighters alive.

'Are you saying, Louisa, don't rubbish your friend? Or don't *kill* him? OK, *gringo*. Put that gun back in your belt. Let's make this a fair fight.'

'Fair?' Pete said, the Solingen aimed steadily at him. 'I wouldn't give you a dog's chance. Louisa get your clothes on. I'm going to have to take you by force.'

'No!' she screamed and lunged at his arm.

As she did so, Corral went for his guns. They were halfway from their holsters when Pete hauled his arm up and fired. Ker-ASH! The explosion reverberated through the apartment as Ramón gave a howl of pain and toppled to one knee.

'No, Pete! Please.' She was hanging to him, sobbing, her hair flailing in his face. 'Don't kill him. He's my husband.'

The Texan peered past her at the sweating, dishevelled Corral, half-lying on the carpet, blood seeping through his fingers as he clutched his shattered thigh. Pete raised the revolver to sight on his chest as men's voices echoed outside in the corridor.

'Pete, you mustn't. He's my son's father. I'm pregnant again.'

Pete paused for seconds, his trigger finger tense. All it needed was the slightest pressure. He felt her clinging to him and shuddered. He thrust her aside on the bed. 'You're welcome to him.' He strode over to the big oak door and turned the key in the lock as boots and spurs clattered outside. Somebody began rattling at the handle.

'Tell them it's OK,' he hissed.

Louisa pulled herself together, went to the door and called, 'There's nothing to worry about. Ramón had a little accident.'

There was a puzzled silence outside and Corral roared, 'Yeah. I'm OK. Clear out.' He looked up, pleadingly, at the Texan as he stood over him and relieved him of his guns. 'You hear me? You don't hurt me. I let you go.'

Pete pursed his lips and his dark eyes

glinted as he stared at Louisa. 'This is what you really want, is it? The riches, the security? You want to be wife of the next president?'

She shook her head. 'It's not just that. Maybe I can do something. Perhaps I can help the people.'

'How you gonna help the people when Pancho Villa puts you all up against a wall an' shoots you?'

Louisa flinched. 'That won't happen.' She put out a hand to touch him as he passed, but he brushed by her.

'Don't be so sure.'

He went through the dressing-room, watched by the maid, kicked the doors open and padded round to the far side of the swimming bath. He found his rope, fixed it to a bulwark of rock and tossed it down. He was about to step over when a group of *rurales* appeared below.

'There's somebody up there,' one shouted.

They were the last words he spoke. Pete's Solingen barked and the slug cut through his throat. His companions began firing and Pete ducked back as their bullets whipped about him. There was no way out down there.

Back in the bedroom Louisa was kneeling beside Ramón on the floor. Maybe it wasn't *her* raised the alarm. She looked up, startled, as Corral slipped a pepperbox pistol from inside his sash. His wild shot dislodged Pete's hat. The Texan stamped on his forearm and cracked him viciously across the jaw with his Solingen. A sudden rage surging through him, he pistol-whipped him until he passed out. He pushed the screaming Louisa aside as men in the corridor hammered on the door. They were using their shoulders against it.

Pete picked up the pepperbox in his left. He stood aside from the door, the lock was about to give. There was a crack as it broke and three *rurales* came charging in. The Texan stuck out his leg and sent the first tumbling, the other two tripping over him. As they turned with their guns raised, the

Solingen in Pete's right hand and the pepperbox in his left, flowered flame and sent them sprawling into a frieze of death.

He stepped out into the murky corridors carved out of stone. There was the rattle of spurs, bootheels and shouts coming from two directions. Two more *rurales* appeared at one corner, their revolvers held high and blasting at him. Pete faced their lead which ricocheted all about him. Firing two-handed he sent them spinning into eternity.

More footfalls behind him. Both his revolvers gave ominous clicks. They were empty. He tossed them aside, grabbed a flaming tar torch from the wall, which cast its shadows along the passage, and thrust it into a *rurale's* face as he came around the corner.

'Aaagh!' The man put his hands up to his face and dropped his carbine.

Pete snatched it up, kicked the man aside, torched another charging *rurale*, levered the carbine and put him down.

He ran on lightly having little idea where he was going. More *rurales* noisily descended some stone steps. He put shots into each one as he came into view and they tumbled into a writhing heap. He kept on firing until the magazine was empty. He picked up a fresh carbine and a belt of ammunition and trod through their squelching blood.

He ran on until he reached two heavy doors. When he pushed them open he saw a cigar-smoky banqueting room, guests on their feet, alarmed at the commotion. Girls screamed as they saw the tall blood-streaked peon, a bandolier of bullets across his shoulder, the carbine in his hand. They must have thought he was Villa's vanguard.

'Hold it right there, *muchachos*. The first man to move gets it.' He smiled, an idea occurring to him. 'I would advise you that the monastery is surrounded by revolutionaries. Every man throw down your guns.'

Most, who were armed, did so,

drawing revolvers from holster, and tossing them clattering down. An American drew a new fangled Mauser automatic from inside his coat and carefully placed it on the table. From his eye corner Pete saw a Mexican rancher of some repute thumb the hammer of a big Colt .45. He spun on him and, before he could squeeze the trigger, put a slug between his eyes.

'Anybody else?' The room had gone deathly quiet. They could hear more coarse imprecations and men in spurred boots running towards the main doors to the banqueting hall. 'Hit the floor, all of you.'

As the guests scrambled for cover a group of cream-uniformed *federales* burst in. Pete pumped the Winchester until the 14-slug magazine was emptied and they went down in all directions like ninepins. He picked up the Mauser and finished off two more who were struggling to their knees.

'Thanks,' he said to the American. And, the Mauser in his fist, he climbed through the debris of bodies.

'Look out!' A blonde Yankee woman involuntarily screamed.

He ducked down as a bullet nearly parted his hair, spun around and aimed two-handed at the *federale* who had fired at his back. Unck! The man grunted, and slumped back.

'Thanks again,' Pete said, glancing at the American blonde. 'Wish I had time to get acquainted, but these folks are after my blood.'

He darted away from more sounds of pursuit, found himself in the monastery's great kitchen, and pushed through greasy-faced cooks, who stood aside to let him pass. A side door opened and a fat-gutted *rurale* stepped in. Pete caught him by his bandana and sent him hurtling and clattering into a pile of soup tureens.

Exiting through the side door he was suddenly out in the night. *Rurales* were running back and forth in the courtyard, not sure what was happening, calling up to the guards on the battlements. They seemed to think a full-scale invasion of Villa-istas was at hand. There was a confusion of horses and coaches waiting to take their owners home, but the big gates were solidly barred.

'Shee-it!' he hissed, at a loss to know how to escape. And then he spied a door, iron-bound, with a skull and crossbones painted on it, signifying explosives. 'Just what I need.' He shot through the padlock with the Mauser and stepped down into a cellar. He struck a match and lit a hurricane lamp. There were barrels of gunpowder, fuse wires, and sticks of dynamite. He broke open a crate and stuck some candle-rods of dynamite in his sash. He got hold of a barrel of gunpowder, fixed a fuse wire, and hefted it bodily back up the stairs, hoping against hope that nobody took a shot at him. He carried it through the semi-darkness towards the parked carriages. Because of his peon outfit nobody took much notice of him. He could have been just a servant with a barrel of wine. *Rurales* shouted at each other and ran past into the main buildings.

There was a feisty-looking black Arab gelding arching his neck and stomping his hooves nervously in the shafts of a light buggy. Pete deposited the barrel in the back and lit the fuse. He leaped into the driving seat, released the brake, and urged him towards the big gates. 'Giddap there!' he shouted. The Arab skittered through the other carriages and pranced towards the gate. Pete hauled him in as a guard on a platform at the top of the gates shouted at him to get back.

Pete jumped down the far side, drew a knife and hacked through the leather traces. When he saw the buggy tight up against the gates, the barrel of gunpowder, the smouldering fuse, the guard screamed out, 'What you doing?' and began firing. Pete raised the Mauser and sent him spinning and catapulting to the ground. He glanced, somewhat anxiously, at the fuse. There were still a few seconds to go. More guards were running along the battlements towards him. He used the fuse-end to light a stick of dynamite and hurled it at them. It exploded, sending heads and limbs disintegrating in all directions.

Pete caught hold of the terrified Arab and swung aboard. He raced back up the courtyard, firing the Mauser point-blank at anybody who got in the way. He paused behind a main building, calming the frightened Arab as the main gates were blown from their hinges in a spectacular display, blown to smithereens.

There was a piece of discarded rope on the cobbles. Pete reached for it and made a makeshift hackamore for the gelding. He hooked it around his arm and slowly took another match from his tin box. A crowd of *rurales* had tumbled out of the main building and were staring at the shattered main portal, as if expecting Villa to come charging through. Pete carefully struck a match, lit a dynamite stick and tossed it at them. He didn't wait to watch the carnage.

Bareback on the black gelding, he whipped it with the rope end and went charging towards the gates as bullets ripped through his clothing. Head down, hanging low, he galloped through, and was away into the night. As he sensed the taste of freedom he gave a wild, ululating, part-Reb, part Comanche yell, 'Yeehaugh'. The wind rippled through the Arab's mane and he went charging on, back towards the shepherd's shack.

'Whee-yew!' he said, as he drew in. 'How the hell did I git outa there?'

★ ★ ★

The Arab was a spirited little beast who had plenty of go in him. By riding him, and resting the other mustang, he reckoned he could put plenty of space between them and the monastery by morning. He had changed back into his civilian suit, his boots and a battered trilby hat. He spurred on hard through the night, following the north star. There was a long way to go across the Sonoran desert, a long way to the invisible line of the *frontera*. But he reckoned he could get a good head start on any pursuit.

He would probably have to evade *rurale* border patrols, the *bandidos*, smugglers and rustlers who infested the mountains both sides of the frontier, maybe even renegade Apaches. Once over the line he could breathe easy, but there would still be a long way to go before he reached Tombstone.

At dawn he paused in a dried-up arroyo and dug down with a stick until he found a sandy drop of water for the horses. He slapped the Arab and sent him running, leaving him to his own devices. His trail might put a pursuer off the scent. He tightened the cinch on his mustang and swung into the saddle, pulled his hat brim down across his eyes against the glare of the rising sun. He had a canteen of water, a bag of flour, a blanket and a good rifle. Straight-backed, he set off at a steady lope across the seemingly unending expanse of cactus and rocky scrub towards the distant mountains. He had always been a lucky son-of-a-gun, though he couldn't say the same for anybody who got in his way. He put the killings behind him. Somewhere out there there was a new life.

13

Black Pete Bowen lay in snug bearskin rugs beside the central fire of the wooden wigwam-like lodge he had built on the Sourwater River in northern Montana. He had built it like that to please his squaw, Left-Hand Woman. It was cosy, if kinda smoky. He could see the stars through the central smoke hole. He smoothed Left-Hand's silky black hair as she snuggled into him. Several years had passed since he was south of the border, but whenever he herded his cattle into Miles City he would put on his new spectacles and take a look at the news sheets. Pancho Villa hadn't done his cause a lot of good with the Americans by shooting up the border town of Columbus and killing sixteen civilians. A US expeditionary force had been sent after him. The war in Mexico ebbed and flowed, President Diaz throwing his federal might against the revolutionaries, who were warring among themselves. Later he read that Diaz had fled as the revolutionary troops entered Mexico City. There was a picture in the paper of the chubby, smiling Pancho Villa, in his leather boots and *generalissimo*'s jacket sitting alongside Emiliano Zapata, among their men. Pete's heart soared with the elation of those days when he rode into a newly captured garrison followed by a horde of yelling shoeless ones.

The next time he rode into Three Forks he saw a news item that suggested things weren't going so well for his old chum Pancho. The crafty General Huerta had had President Madero assassinated. Pancho had been sentenced to death and thrown in jail. With the usual Villa panache he had escaped and made his way by horseback back to Chihuahua where he was rumoured to be gathering his forces together for another rebellion.[1] It was all very confusing, but that was the way things were in Mexico. At least Diaz and Ramón Corral had gone. Mexico had the beginnings of some sort of freedom.

'What happened to that man Corral and the girl, Louisa, you tol' me 'bout?' Left-Hand murmured, as she fingered his thigh.

'Hell knows. Guess, like always, the rats deserted the sinkin' ship. Probably took their diamonds with 'em. They'll be living in luxurious exile someplace, I guess.'

He lay and thought about those far off days for a while. What had they proved? The howl of a wolf pack came echoing to him from the woods outside. 'Sounds like they're out tonight in full

---

[1] Villa found his own personal bullet years later. Fifty-six of them, in fact, riddled his body when he, too, was assassinated.

cry after my herd,' he said, getting to his feet. 'I better go take a look.'

'No, Pete. Stay. I was just — ' Left-Hand hung on to his leg. 'Why don't you get some of the boys to go out? You're the boss.'

He pushed his fingers through his thinning hair and grinned ruefully. 'You think I could get Curly and those lazy bastards outa the bunkhouse on a night like this? No, they're my cows. I better go. I gotta warn them wolves it ain't wise to come nosing round this way.'

He pulled on his fur-lined macinaw and Stetson and went to look into the adjoining cabin where his ten-year-old son and nine-year-old daughter lay tucked up. He stroked their dark hair and smiled, a warm tenderness flooding through him. It was good to have a family. It was good not to be on the lam any more. He was a respected rancher these days.

'They're asleep,' he said, as he scratched his grey-flecked beard, and reached for the gold-plated Browning rifle from the rack. 'I won't be long.'

'You want me to ride with you, Pete?'

'No, you stay where you are,' he grinned. 'I'm gonna be needin' you nice and warm when I git back.'

He stepped out of the 'wigwam' door, went to the stable and saddled his grey. He rode out across an expanse of crisp pristine snow, through the shadows of the dark pines swathing the hills. A cold bright moon illumined his land in a purple glow. He held the rifle in his gloved hand, listening for the distant howl of the pack. It was a hard life being a cowboy, but one he loved. It always would be.

THE END

FIGHTING RAMROD
Charles N. Heckelmann

Most men would have cut their losses, but Frazer counted the bullets in his guns and said he'd soak the range in blood before he'd give up another inch of what was his.

LONE GUN
Eric Allen

Smoke Blackbird had been away too long. The Lequires had seized the Blackbird farm, forcing the Indians and settlers off, and no one seemed willing to fight! He had to fight alone.

THE THIRD RIDER
Barry Cord

Mel Rawlins wasn't going to let anything stand in his way. His father was murdered, his two brothers gone. Now Mel rode for vengeance.

ARIZONA DRIFTERS
W. C. Tuttle

When drifting Dutton and Lonnie Steelman decide to become partners they find that they have a common enemy in the formidable Thurston brothers.

TOMBSTONE
Matt Braun

Wells Fargo paid Luke Starbuck to outgun the silver-thieving stagecoach gang at Tombstone. Before long Luke can see the only thing bearing fruit in this eldorado will be the gallows tree.

HIGH BORDER RIDERS
Lee Floren

Buckshot McKee and Tortilla Joe cut the trail of a border tough who was running Mexican beef into Texas. They stopped the smuggler in his tracks.

BRETT RANDALL, GAMBLER
E. B. Mann

Larry Day had the choice of running away from the law or of assuming a dead man's place. No matter what he decided he was bound to end up dead.

THE GUNSHARP
William R. Cox

The Eggerleys weren't very smart. They trained their sights on Will Carney and Arizona's biggest blood bath began.

THE DEPUTY OF SAN RIANO
Lawrence A. Keating and
Al. P. Nelson

When a man fell dead from his horse, Ed Grant was spotted riding away from the scene. The deputy sheriff rode out after him and came up against everything from gunfire to dynamite.

FARGO: MASSACRE RIVER
John Benteen

The ambushers up ahead had now blocked the road. Fargo's convoy was a jumble, a perfect target for the insurgents' weapons!

SUNDANCE: DEATH IN THE LAVA
John Benteen

The Modoc's captured the wagon train and its cargo of gold. But now the halfbreed they called Sundance was going after it . . .

HARSH RECKONING
Phil Ketchum

Five years of keeping himself alive in a brutal prison had made Brand tough and careless about who he gunned down . . .

FARGO: PANAMA GOLD
John Benteen

With foreign money behind him, Buckner was going to destroy the Panama Canal before it could be completed. Fargo's job was to stop Buckner.

FARGO:
THE SHARPSHOOTERS
John Benteen

The Canfield clan, thirty strong were raising hell in Texas. Fargo was tough enough to hold his own against the whole clan.

PISTOL LAW
Paul Evan Lehman

Lance Jones came back to Mustang for just one thing — revenge! Revenge on the people who had him thrown in jail.

HELL RIDERS
Steve Mensing

Wade Walker's kid brother, Duane, was locked up in the Silver City jail facing a rope at dawn. Wade was a ruthless outlaw, but he was smart, and he had vowed to have his brother out of jail before morning!

DESERT OF THE DAMNED
Nelson Nye

The law was after him for the murder of a marshal — a murder he didn't commit. Breen was after him for revenge — and Breen wouldn't stop at anything . . . blackmail, a frameup . . . or murder.

DAY OF THE COMANCHEROS
Steven C. Lawrence

Their very name struck terror into men's hearts — the Comancheros, a savage army of cutthroats who swept across Texas, leaving behind a bloodstained trail of robbery and murder.

SUNDANCE: SILENT ENEMY
John Benteen

A lone crazed Cheyenne was on a personal war path. They needed to pit one man against one crazed Indian. That man was Sundance.

LASSITER
Jack Slade

Lassiter wasn't the kind of man to listen to reason. Cross him once and he'll hold a grudge for years to come — if he let you live that long.

LAST STAGE TO GOMORRAH
Barry Cord

Jeff Carter, tough ex-riverboat gambler, now had himself a horse ranch that kept him free from gunfights and card games. Until Sturvesant of Wells Fargo showed up.

McALLISTER ON THE COMANCHE CROSSING
Matt Chisholm

The Comanche, McAllister owes them a life — and the trail is soaked with the blood of the men who had tried to outrun them before.

QUICK-TRIGGER COUNTRY
Clem Colt

Turkey Red hooked up with Curly Bill Graham's outlaw crew. But wholesale murder was out of Turk's line, so when range war flared he bucked the whole border gang alone . . .

CAMPAIGNING
Jim Miller

Ambushed on the Santa Fe trail, Sean Callahan is saved by two Indian strangers. But there'll be more lead and arrows flying before the band join Kit Carson against the Comanches.

GUNSLINGER'S RANGE
Jackson Cole

Three escaped convicts are out for revenge. They won't rest until they put a bullet through the head of the dirty snake who locked them behind bars.

RUSTLER'S TRAIL
Lee Floren

Jim Carlin knew he would have to stand up and fight because he had staked his claim right in the middle of Big Ike Outland's best grass.

THE TRUTH ABOUT SNAKE RIDGE
Marshall Grover

The troubleshooters came to San Cristobal to help the needy. For Larry and Stretch the turmoil began with a brawl and then an ambush.

WOLF DOG RANGE
Lee Floren

Will Ardery would stop at nothing, unless something stopped him first — like a bullet from Pete Manly's gun.

DEVIL'S DINERO
Marshall Grover

Plagued by remorse, a rich old reprobate hired the Texas Trouble-shooters to deliver a fortune in greenbacks to each of his victims.

GUNS OF FURY
Ernest Haycox

Dane Starr, alias Dan Smith, wanted to close the door on his past and hang up his guns, but people wouldn't let him.

DONOVAN
Elmer Kelton

Donovan was supposed to be dead. Uncle Joe Vickers had fired off both barrels of a shotgun into the vicious outlaw's face as he was escaping from jail. Now Uncle Joe had been shot — in just the same way.

CODE OF THE GUN
Gordon D. Shirreffs

MacLean came riding home, with saddle tramp written all over him, but sewn in his shirt-lining was an Arizona Ranger's star.

GAMBLER'S GUN LUCK
Brett Austen

Gamblers seldom live long. Parker was a hell of a gambler. It was his life — or his death . . .

ORPHAN'S PREFERRED
Jim Miller

Sean Callahan answers the call of the Pony Express and fights Indians and outlaws to get the mail through.

DAY OF THE BUZZARD
T. V. Olsen

All Val Penmark cared about was getting the men who killed his wife.

THE MANHUNTER
Gordon D. Shirreffs

Lee Kershaw knew that every Rurale in the territory was on the lookout for him. But the offer of $5,000 in gold to find five small pieces of leather was too good to turn down.